Sydnee A. Nelson

Blood of the Sire

The Raceling Chronicles: Book 1

Front cover image by Alice Palmer.
Illustrations by Devin Nelson.

Printed by Blurb, Inc., in the United States of America.

First printing edition 2019.

www.sydneeanelson.com

Dedications:

This book is dedicated to the ones who supported me for this incredibly long journey. Those of you who have stuck around for ten years, listening to me tell you everything about the story before I even started writing it down, I cannot thank you enough.

To my parents for keeping me going. To my beloved grandmother that listened to me rant. To my brothers that pushed me to work harder. And to my sister, my best friend, who helped shape this world of mine with her own love and teenage angst.

Thank you for ten years of support. Here's to twenty more.

-Sydnee Alyse Nelson-

In loving memory of Twix the rat.
Aug. 17th 2016 - Dec. 23rd 2018

The Hide, illustrated by Devin Nelson

Chapter 1

Blood and Venom

A slap sent her flying face-first to the ground,

blood sprinkling from her lips onto the stone. She

barely had time to lift her head before the fist

connected with her cheek, slamming her face back

into the floor and cracking the rock. She coughed

heavily, blood from her cheek and lips splattering

across the ground to join the puddles of blood and

piss left by other prisoners. She lifted her head to look

at her tormentor. His ugly, snarling face was

illuminated by the dancing firelight from the brazier

beside him and the single candle on the lone table behind her. He was tall and broad-shouldered, his face covered in small scars that were barely visible in the dim candlelight. He bared his white teeth.

"Talk, Miss Relix," a voice from behind the man said. Mayline looked past the large man in front of her. The one sitting in the chair she had previously occupied was tall and thin, his angular face defined sharply by the shadows in the candle-light. She spat out blood onto the stone in front of her once again, wincing as she picked herself up slightly. The smell of roasted pig drifted up to her nose. She looked down at her burned side, oozing out a white liquid that congealed around the wound and fizzled around the

skin. The rod which was used to burn her was pushed

near her face. She looked up at the man in front of her

again, noting the yellow in his eyes betraying his

Primary as Werewolf, and snarled at him.

"Hurt me all you like, Prime, I won't talk."

The poker was smacked across her shoulder, digging

into the flesh easily. It cut deeply into the meat of her

shoulder, tearing muscles and scorching off blood-

flow. She screamed, her throat feeling raw. The

guttural sound echoed around the room until the rod

was pulled away, pulling off sections of skin with the

motion. Mayline dropped to the ground again, her

hand scraping against the rock beneath her. She could feel the venom in her blood beginning to attempt the healing process, more white liquid oozing from her shoulder. She bared her teeth and grunted as she hauled herself to a sitting position. She growled deep in her throat, stood, and charged at her tormentors.

Her head jerked forward as she was grabbed from behind, killing her momentum and forcing her back to the ground. The thin man caught her hair in one hand, jerking her head back to expose her throat, and clenched her arms behind her back with the other. She was on her knees then, wholly exposed to the large Werewolf in front of her.

"Now, now, Raceling, do not make this any harder on you than it has to be. We can make the rest of your short life much more comfortable if you just tell us where your friends are hiding," the thin man said from behind her. Mayline winced as her shoulder was pulled, the wound opening again under the scabs formed by the venom in her blood. She hissed and bared her teeth in defiance.

"You want the location? Give me that blade, I'll carve it into your corpse!"

With a growl, the man wrenched her backward and toward the chair. The bigger one stood over the chair, holding the metal spike over a fire lit

in the brazier. The metal was already glowing white.

Mayline struggled, dread clenching in her stomach.

Her eyes widened as she was dragged closer to the

fire.

"No- no, please!" She lost all bravado, her

voice rising in pitch. She was shoved into the chair,

and the thin man held her arms behind it. The spike

was brought around in front of her. Mayline stared at

the white-hot metal and clenched her teeth. "Fine."

The thin man leaned in until his rancid breath brushed

across her neck.

"Sorry, what was that?" he asked, his voice mocking her. Mayline shut her eyes and dropped her head in defeat.

"I said fine," she hissed, a little louder. The bigger man grinned, his face was ugly in the expression.

Her arms were released, and the thin man came around to kneel beside her. He smiled kindly at her, but Mayline knew he wasn't genuine.

"Well, then, was that so hard?" he asked. He put a hand on her cheek, brushing away dirt and blood. "Where are they hiding, little one?" Mayline looked from one silver eye to the other. His Primary

was Changeling. Mayline heaved a breath out,

looking away. Her eyes fell on the pot of fire.

"They... " Fire - spike - Changeling? "Do you

have a map? I can just show you," she said, looking

back at the man. He grinned, his teeth were slightly

pointed.

"Ethio, bring us a map, would you?" he said,

waving a hand at the Werewolf dismissively. Ethio

huffed and dropped the spike into the fire again,

walking through the darkness. Mayline heard a door

shut behind her. The Changeling stood up straight and

moved toward the shadow. She heard things being run around on wood and he came back into the light with a damp cloth and bandages. Mayline watched him suspiciously.

"Now, then, with all this nasty business over with, you can be treated as befits your Race. You might be only a Bloodling, but you are still a Vampire," He said, kneeling in front of her. Mayline saw the gooey liquid on the cloth and shifted.

"Is that-"

"Venom, yes. Kindly donated by a few of our resident Vampires and treated by our Banshee healers

to heal wounds faster," he said. He gently took hold
of her shoulder, carefully dabbing the venom onto the
wound. Mayline hissed, her eyes flashing red in pain.

"I know it hurts, but it will help, I promise."
He sounded almost… genuine.

"What's your name?" she asked. He paused
for a moment and glanced at her.

"I am called Mortar. I've been alive so long, I
have forgotten my true name." Mayline raised an
eyebrow at his response.

"Mortar…? But... weren't you the one who my
platoon was supposed to meet? To get the blueprints

of one of the holds on the surface?" Mortar nodded, not looking at her. "Why did you betray us?" she growled. Mortar shushed her and calmly rubbed the now bloody cloth across her side.

"I did not betray you, child. I was doing as I was told by your superiors. Did you not wonder why you were the only one we took captive while we left your comrades in the woods? Your... leaders... asked me to try and break you, to see if you would betray their secrets under pressure. It seems that they were correct." He gave her a look that made her blood boil.

"You see that rod?" she said, guiding his eyes

to see her foot poised to kick the rod in such a way

that it would have flipped, sending it in his direction.

"And that fire?" In her palm was a rock she had

managed to grab in the scuffle of her being dragged.

It wasn't large, but it was enough to knock over the

fire into the direction of the chair she was in.

"If you had not started to talk, I would have

killed you within minutes. Fire and Changelings don't

mix well, Mortar. Do not ever doubt my loyalty. That

map was a distraction to get one of you out of the

room. I would have to lead you to a completely

different location if one of you didn't leave. I would

have done my best to hold their secrets until my own

death. If anyone's loyalties are questionable, they are

yours, not mine. My superiors do not trust me because

I'm half Vampire. That's the reason for their

suspicions; they are not grounded in truth or

evidence."

Mortar nodded slowly, a small smile forming

on his thin lips.

"So it would seem, my dear, that they were

wrong to doubt you." He looked at her quietly for a

moment as he wrapped the bandages. He sighed and

looked back at his work.

"When Ethio returns with the map, you will

give a location far away from the real one. He will be

eager to get a team together to attack the Racelings. I

will take you to a cell, and when we are moving, you

will escape my grasp. The exit is three flights up. You

will need to be fast. Once they find out you have

escaped me, they will come for you.

"Younger Werewolves have no control over

their change. The full moon rises tonight, and you

will be their target. May Artemis grace you with

speed, my young friend." Mortar placed three fingers

to her brow and muttered something in a language she

did not know, but assumed was Greek. "Olympus

knows you will need it." He returned to tending her

wounds.

When the last bandage was secured, and she could feel the healing of her broken skin and muscles beginning, the door opened again, and Ethio walked in, grinning like mad.

"My little brother is going through his first change tonight, Mortar. The King is allowing them the use of the woods on the surface to hunt and enjoy the moonlight." Ethio handed Mortar the rolled up map with a nod. Mortar chuckled and stood up, unrolling the map.

"Once we are finished here, Ethio, you may

join your kin in the moonlight. I will handle escorting

the prisoner to her cell," Mortar said, unrolling the

map and showing the expanse to Mayline. "Now, tell

us, Raceling, where your friends are hiding."

Mayline looked down at the map, trying to

think of a place far enough away to send them that

was still both possible and believable. Send them too

far, however, and they would see through it with ease.

She looked across the map, looking over the expanse

of country borders and isles. The map was far from

complete, showing nothing to past east Ukraine. She

would have to find something far, far away from her

people's home. The Hide must be protected. But

where? Where could she send them?

"I can't see the landmark on this map, but it's in this general area." She pointed to Alberta, Canada. It was far enough away that the Hide would be safe, but across the continent from the actual location was still close enough to be a headquarters for the North American Racelings. Mortar nodded and gestured to Ethio.

"Go. Tell the others. I will deal with her. Enjoy your Moon Night, my friend." Ethio nodded and grinned evilly down at Mayline.

"I hope you get to live the rest of your

miserable half-life knowing you've condemned your kind to extinction," he said, eyes gleaming. Mayline glared at him as he walked out of the room, chuckling to himself as he went. She growled, her teeth throbbing slightly. She wanted so badly to clench her jaw around his jugular. Mortar placed a hand on her unbandaged shoulder, keeping her in place until the door was shut.

"Now then… How to get you out without blowing my cover… Quite the question, aye, Bloodling?" he asked. She glared at him, cracking her jaw.

"Isn't it obvious? I wound you, escape, and lead the guards on a merry chase to a fort that doesn't exist in an effort to warn a headquarters that isn't there. You're a bit slow on the uptake, aren't you?" she said, mocking him with a smirk. He glowered at her and turned his hand upward to point at the ceiling.

"And tell me, oh great Mayline, how do you plan on maneuvering through the maze of hallways, getting to the surface? Have you forgotten as well that the forest will be full of Prime Werewolves? How do you expect to sneak anywhere when your scent is so obviously tainted with human? You'd be lucky to get to the end of this hallway alive. Try again, little one.

And do make this one a good one. We do not have all night."

Mayline glared at the Prime before her, her body already half-healed. He had been right. She would be lucky to get through the fortress alive. But she did not need to make it out alive. She just needed to make it out. She was only halfway living anyway. And a half-life was better than no life. Mortar was watching her, seeing the wheels in her head turning through the expression on her face.

"You're right, of course." He smirked in victory at her acquiescence.

Suddenly, with a twist of her foot, she brought the rod up and into her hands. With a loud roar, she swung it at Mortar's head. It connected before he had time to react and he hit the floor with a heavy thud. He groaned, looking through bleary eyes at Mayline.

"You're right. Too bad I never listen. Thanks for your help. Good luck." With that, she turned and opened the door.

Chapter 2

Mortar and Pestle

The hallway was dark and damp like any

dungeon should have been. There were dozens of

doors lining the walls, each one most likely hiding

either prisoners or guards. The doors were wooden

with iron bindings and iron locks on each handle.

Each one had a torch beside it, lighting the dimness

from their iron sconces. The hallway was dim, but she

could see that everything was nearly identical. How

could she possibly navigate? She'd have to be careful.

She could not risk letting out any other prisoners or

being seen.

Turning to look around, she noticed the markings for each door seemed coded. Every other door had a different marking, matching the door two before it. She examined them, trying to find the pattern. Across from her, there was a marking different from the others. She assumed it was to another hallway. Mayline ran toward it, wincing as her still healing wounds reopened with the movement, blood and venom dripping from her and onto the floor. Behind her, she could hear people talking, and then Mortar's voice shouting. She cursed and slammed through the door. It was another hallway, but this one was much shorter and had a staircase leading up to the next level at the end. She heaved herself up the stairs, reaching the next level.

They were stupid for keeping her so close to the next floor.

Mayline quickened her pace as she heard them behind her, enemies within their own borders, and turned swiftly to the right. She vaguely remembered the way back. Coming around a corner, she skidded to a halt, heart beating heavily as fear seeped into her bones.

It was a full moon. And there were three

chained and mangy Werewolves looking at her with black, beady eyes, snarling and growling for the blood dripping from her shoulder. All three of them were young and covered in the blood of their first change. Idly, her mind wondered if Ethio's brother was among them. Her hope plummeted. She was in no condition to fight three of the one species that almost matched her own in speed, even if they were young and inexperienced.

"Blood on the floor! She went this way," a voice behind her shouted, the sound of pounding feet getting closer. She had to get out of there, but with the only other way blocked, there were no options. She had to make a stand, or hide. Fighting would only get

her killed faster; hiding it was then.

Gingerly removing her shirt, Mayline tossed it

toward the Werewolves, watching with disgust as they

attacked it as if it were her actual flesh. With this

distraction, she looked around for a way to hide and

quickly noticed the beams running across the ceiling

of the hallway, just barely lit from the single torch in

the area where she stood.

Taking a deep breath, preparing for the pain to

come, Mayline crouched down and curled her body to

give herself maximum momentum. Just as the sound

of her pursuers turning the corner reached her ears,

Mayline hurled herself up to the beam, reaching out

with both hands to grab hold. Her fingers clutched at

the ancient wood and pain lanced through her body as

her shoulder and side were strained. She pulled

herself up with difficulty but managed without giving

away her position to either the wolves in front of her

or the ones chasing her.

She watched as the men came to her section

and started searching for her. One pointed to the

wolves, who were still tearing into her shirt.

"Vic, do you think she got passed them?

Maybe they injured her more and took her blouse?"

he asked. Mayline smirked.

"No one could make it passed three

Werewolves on the night of a full moon in a space

this small and live, Andrew. It's impossible!" another

shouted. The growing argument was cut short by a

silky smooth male voice, cutting through the air like a

sword.

"And why not?"

The men fell silent and turned to stare at

Mortar who had materialized out of the shadows like

a wraith, venom dripping down his chin to heal the

cut she had given him. The men cowered before him, parting as he made his way toward the three wolves, showing no hesitation at all as they turned to growl and snap their slobbering jowls at him. Mayline held her breath, waiting for him to either give her away or lead them off.

"Injured though she may be, Relix is still a Raceling. She has the abilities of her Race. She shares the venom of her Sire, Demitri. Is it not true that even Halfbreeds can retain some of their Sire's abilities? When she was tested, supposedly the results said her Race-level is twice as high as the original Raceling, Peace himself. Would that not make her stronger than the average Raceling?" Mortar turned to the men,

some of which were beginning to glance at each other

in uncertainty. Mayline tried to stifle a laugh with her

hand but barely managed it. The cowards got nervous

from just the mention of the long lost Raceling,

Peace.

Mortar turned and gestured to the wolves, who

had still raved and lashed out toward him during his

speech.

"Any decent Raceling could have gotten

through this easily, even as injured and starved as

Relix is. We are wasting time here. Follow her!" he

yelled and turned away. As the fear-stricken men started attempting to calm the now enraged wolves enough to move passed, Mayline caught the eyes of Mortar as he glanced up at her position. She held her breath, and he smiled thinly. He sent her a wink and continued onwards, Mayline smirked. He had proven that, at least for now, she could trust him.

The crowd of Primes had calmed the wolves enough for them to get through, and began running down the hallway, away from her hiding place. When they were completely out of sight, Mayline shut her eyes, leaned to the side, and dropped onto the floor with a whisper.

She straightened, wincing at the pain in her side and shoulder. She turned back to the way she had come and nearly hit her nose on Mortar's chest. She backed up slightly and smirked.

"Nice cover, big guy," she said. He chuckled and raised his hand to his head, bowing slightly.

"Nice swing, little girl," he said. Mayline rolled her eyes and crossed her arms, fighting back her pained expression at the movement of her shoulder.

"Do you think you've given yourself enough cover to help me get out, then?" He covered her mouth, looking around the small, dim hallway as if the walls could hear her. When he was satisfied that the walls, in fact, did not have ears, he nodded and gestured for him to follow her.

"This way. But be careful, there might still be enemies lurking about," he said and beckoned her toward the end of the hall. As she followed him, the wolves' angry howls and barks growing fainter with distance, Mayline could not help but shiver. She was not one to put her trust blindly in another, let alone a Prime of any Race, but her own inadequacy had lead to this. She was not privy to the inner parts of the headquarters for the armies of Hell. As much as it went against her basic instincts, human and Raceling,

she would have to follow this stranger.

"You said you could not remember being

called anything but Mortar. Why?" He glanced over

his shoulder at her and then looked straight ahead

again.

"It's been so long since anyone called me

anything other than Mortar. I've come to know myself

by that name as well," he said. Mayline frowned.

"You don't remember your human name?" she

asked. Mortar laughed and shook his head.

"No. I do not remember any of my human

existence. Sometimes I wish I did, but it is the times when I remember just how old I actually am, that I am glad I cannot remember if I even had a family to miss," he said. She nodded solemnly.

"I wish my memory was obscured like that." He looked back at her as they turned a corner, heading into a more well-lit area of the dungeonesque halls.

"Surely, you are not that old? You do not look the age when Racelings freeze in time," he said. Mayline shook her head.

"I was changed five years ago. But the night I was murdered-" she glanced at him, "for there is truly no other way to describe it - I was forced to watch as

a pack of Prime Vampires slaughtered and drained my

parents and brother." She looked straight ahead to

avoid meeting his pitying eyes.

"There are times I wish I did not have the

memory of a family to mourn for," she murmured. He

nodded, his eyes turning to fix upon a point in the

distance of the hall.

"Understandable, given your… circumstances.

I give condolences for your loss, both your family

and your humanity," he said. Mayline graced him

with a small smile, letting her own pain bleed into her

eyes even as he did the same. Then he stopped

abruptly beside a rotted, old wooden door.

"I am afraid this is where we part, Miss Relix.

It was a pleasure," he said and bowed. Mayline

nodded and sighed.

"Do you have any messages you wish to

convey, while I'm heading that way?" Mayline asked.

Mortar grinned, his overly white teeth gleaming in the

torchlight. He reached into his coat and pulled out a

scroll of parchment.

"As a matter of fact, I do. All the information I

wish to give your leaders is in the scroll. Do be

careful not to lose it, it was too dangerous to make

more than one copy," he said and handed it to her

with a grin. Mayline nodded in acknowledgment and

tucked the scroll safely into her belt.

"Thank you for your assistance, Mortar. It will

not go unpaid," she said. Mortar smiled and shook his

head.

"Miss Relix, just being able to meet you was

payment enough for me. Safe travels and may your

blade never dull," he said. Mayline grinned and

opened the door.

"And may your sword stay sharp, Mortar, you

are a friend to the Racelings," she said and slipped

out into the bright sunlight of the world of freedom.

As the door slowly closed behind her, Mortar's

smile faded. He turned and walked back into the

dungeons, melting into the darkness.

Where he had once stood, three figures

emerged from the shadows. The one in the center

stood half a head taller than the other men, his hair

seemed to drip blood from its auburn tips, and his

eyes shimmered silver. He wore a suit of burgundy

with a black waistcoat, both tailored around his large

white wings, and his shoes let off a shine as the black

leather moved. His red lips turned into a sinister

smirk.

"Master Hellios, the Raceling is getting

away!" the shorter of the other men cried. Hellios

raised a hand toward the door.

"If you think she is important enough to

capture once again, Jashin, then, by all means, take

Charles and attempt to bring her back. I, however, am

more concerned with the traitor in our midst," he said

and turned away. "But if catching the little pest is

important to you, then I shall not stop you. But leave

now, if you want to catch up to her. She is a quick

little thing," he said, tossing the words over his shoulder as he walked away into the blackness. Jashin growled, red eyes narrowed, and smacked Charles on the shoulder lightly.

"Let's go get the Raceling, then," he said, and the two Vampires followed Mayline through the door and into the harsh light of day.

The hunters now had their prey.

<u>Chapter 3</u>

Hunters in the Night

Feet pounded the dry earth, turning up the undergrowth of a forest floor.

Faster. Must run faster.

Two pursuers gaining ground.

Go, Mayline, *go*!

Mayline ran as hard as she could with her injuries. Her feet hit the dirt lightly, pushing her faster until her heart pounded in her chest and her breathing was ragged from exertion and pain.

Behind her, Charles and Jashin were gaining ground. The wind whipped her hair into her eyes as she glanced backward at them for an instant. Tree branches snapped against her face as she ran onward, heading toward where her instincts said was safe.

She was too injured to risk direct confrontation. If she could get out of their line of sight, she might be able to catch them by surprise. An idea suddenly came to her, and she gritted her teeth. It had to work. Turning on her toes, flipping herself to face the oncoming Primes, just as they both passed her, Mayline skidded to a halt.

Jashin and Charles skidded, their momentum pushing them farther away from their prey. Mayline took the opportunity to leap into the air and catch a low hanging branch, heaving herself into the tree. By the time her enemies had halted and turned, she was already well hidden inside the branches.

Jashin turned a slow circle, scanning the surrounding trees for any sign of a Raceling hiding behind them. Charles leaped into a tree, across from Mayline's hiding place, and sniffed the air. His red eyes scanned the trees, searching for movement.

Mayline held her breath. She waited until

Charles had turned to look the other way, before

leaping to a different branch and swinging herself to

another tree.

She slowly made her way to the trunk, careful

of making any noise. Jashin turned abruptly and

hissed as a noise came from a bush below her hiding

place. He growled in frustration when the small

squirrel ran away from the three predators. Mayline

glanced to the branch above Charles. If she could

just…

She leaped toward the branch.

Her feet landed silently on the branch, the

leaves rustling only slightly, lost in the loud growls

from below her as she slid until she was hanging

upside down from the branch. Mayline held her

breath and waited several long minutes. Finally,

Jashin turned away from Charles, providing the

perfect opportunity. Mayline dropped from her branch

and latched her legs around Charles's neck. She cut

off his scream by twisting her body to throw him

from the tree, her claw-like fingers ripping into his

flesh from his throat to his wrist.

He dropped like a dead weight into a bush on

the forest floor, the noise causing Jashin to whirl

round and growl, but Mayline had already leaped

from her perch into another tree, higher up and away from him.

Charles stood, his dark blood dripping from the long wounds the young Raceling had inflicted. He hissed and pointed upward, unable to speak as his throat slowly mended. Jashin glanced up, noting the darkening sky.

She dropped down a few branches and watched Jashin leap into the branches below her, glaring in her direction. She kept perfectly still, not daring to even breathe. But it was not enough. Jashin lunged toward her, hands outstretched to claw at her skin. Mayline tried to jump away, but he caught her

leg and threw her downward.

Her back slammed against the tree trunk, and

she shrieked in pain, her vision going dark. She

blinked, trying to focus. She had to get up, she had to

move. But she was not even able to twitch a finger.

Her back pulsed with pain.

Jashin and Charles made their way to her,

growling. Charles held his hand to his throat, keeping

the pieces together so they would heal faster, his teeth

gnashing together. Jashin, reached for Mayline,

yanking her upward by the collar of her shirt, and

thrusting her against the tree. The pain ran up her spine until it went numb. Jashin's putrid breath assaulted her nostrils as he leaned toward his captive, hissing.

"You put up a good fight, little Raceling, but not good enough," he growled. Charles gurgled in agreement. Mayline tried to speak, to say something witty and biting, but the hand around her throat hindered her speech. Mayline forced her numb arms to move, sending pain through her entire body. She managed to clench her fists around Jashin's stained sleeve. His cruel smile twisted into a snarl and the fingers around her neck tightened. Her eyes rolled back into her head, and her breathing weakened.

"Say goodnight, scum-blood bitch." Then the world went black.

A howl pierced the air, and Charles and Jashin spun around. The limp body of Mayline fell to the forest floor in a heap behind them.

A burst of green light shot from the tree line and hit Charles in the chest, knocking him back into a tree, his chest smoking and showing his pale, white collar bone. Jashin spun around toward where the light had come from just in time to see a tall, lean woman with long brown hair pulled back into a tight ponytail and holding a long staff with blades on each

end. The end of her staff stabbed through his shoulder

and locked him onto a tree behind him. Behind her, a

figure covered in dark red hair darted forward. The

figure launched itself onto Charles and pinned him

down, holding him there to buy her companion time.

Jashin gripped the staff and ripped it out of the

ground, crying out in pain as it left his shoulder. He

tossed it away and stood, facing the woman who was

standing protectively over Mayline's prone form. He

growled and leaped toward her. She jumped at him

and they connected in the air and Jashin was forced

back to the ground by the small woman. He used her

momentum to roll her off of him, pushing her with his

feet. She flipped and landed smoothly, even as Jashin

rolled back to his feet and pounced at her. She spun

around, and Jashin reached for her throat, but his

hands passed right through her and hit the dirt. He

spluttered and turned to look over his shoulder. The

woman seemed to be standing there, but as he looked

closer he saw the landscape through her, and he

realized her scent was so faint it was barely even

there. He snarled.

"Banshee!"

The woman smirked and picked up her staff,

sinking into a defensive position in front of the still unmoving Mayline.

"Hello!" she said in a sing-song tone. "Back away now, boys."

Jashin growled and rolled to his feet, and pushed himself toward her, ready to grab the only solid thing on her person. His hands reached for her staff, and she tried to jump backward but was too slow. He yanked the staff, and she was jerked to the side and forced to the ground. Her form was suddenly corporeal as her head was knocked against the dirt. His substantial body pinned her to the ground, the staff pressed against her chest.

"Banshees have always been weaker than us!" Jashin hissed, grinning in triumph. The woman grinned and licked her lips.

"And yet I can still beat Vamps like you before breakfast," she said, and he laughed. Then her mouth opened, widening and widening until her jaw looked as though it might break. Jashin staggered back as he saw the beginnings of flames licking at the woman's teeth. She took a deep breath as she got to her knees, twisting to face Jashin as he pushed himself backward over the ground in a panic. He screamed as she exhaled an orange and red jet of flame, bursting around her glistening white teeth and shooting toward the Vampire.

Jashin shrieked in terror as the flames reached his feet, melting his shoes and burning his ankles. The smell of tainted sweet blood filled the air and clung to the woman's tongue as she halted the flow of fire. Jashin screamed loudly, trying to pat out the flames that climbed up his body as though it had a mind of its own. His hands caught fire, and he attempted to put them out, only serving to allow them to spread up his arms. The woman stood and watched as he burned, slowly. Then she raised her hand and water gushed from her palm, her lips moving in a chant.

Steam rose from his body as the flames were quenched by the waters from her spell. When the steam dissipated, the quivering form of Jashin was revealed. Burned flesh covered him, twisting and turning in an intricate pattern. Half of his face was covered in the swirling burns, smoldering with red and yellow embers. Jashin, shivering with the pain in his exposed nerves, turned his head slowly to look at the woman. His mouth, trembling, opened.

"Y-you…" his voice cracked. "should have killed me…" His chest heaving with his pained breaths, he grunted and winced with the effort of speaking. The woman shook her head, pointing to Mayline.

"You tortured my friend, showing her no mercy. Death would be a gift to you, Prime. You will live. You will live in pain for the rest of your existence. However long or short that may be." She moved toward the still form of her friend.

"And besides," she paused at his side, looking down at him. "I am not a pointless killer. I am, however, a pointless sadist." She continued walking toward Mayline and picked her up. She turned, looking at her companion.

Charles saw the vibrant green eyes of the girl
crushing his injured chest with her small body, her
teeth bared and her fingers elongated into claws, and
he felt the instinctual fear that comes to Vampires
when faced with their mortal enemies.

The Werewolf girl grinned ferally down at
him as his eyes widened and he struggled to get away.
The girl held up her hand and brought her claws down
through his still healing throat, ripping through his
flesh like butter. Charles thrust his hand up,
attempting to claw at the face that snarled down at

him. The girl knocked it away and pinned his hands down and raised her claws again to attack. Charles rolled himself on top of her pinning her down and growling, baring his teeth at her. She snarled and struggled under him, anger allowing her to throw him off of her and into the tree beside them. She rolled and leaped toward him and clawed at his throat once again, cutting through his shoulder as he rolled away.

"Rae!" The Werewolf girl turned to look at the woman holding Mayline. She stood up from her crouch and bounded towards the woman.

"Jennifer, is she okay?" Rae murmured. The

woman shook her head.

"Her back feels swollen, and she has obviously been tortured. We need to get her to the healers, quickly," she said. Rae nodded and looked back at Charles. His throat was healing slowly, both it and his shoulder seeping out his near black blood and mixing with his clear venom to heal faster. Jashin was in a similar state, his burns seeping his venom and the clear liquid killing the grass under him.

"Alright then. These bastards are taken care of for now, but they won't die. Let's go home." With that, the two women turned and started running toward their home.

The two women ran across a field, Jennifer carrying Mayline in her arms. Rae sprinted beside her, careful to keep her eyes on their backs. They tried to quickly make their way toward their home base, hidden away in the forests of oak and pine. They slowed to a walk as they reached an open plain. Rae moved behind a tree, eyes scanning the open area for movement, while Jennifer stayed back with Mayline.

Nothing moved except the wind pushing the grass to move like water. Rae's bright green eyes darted across the plain as she slowly stepped around the tree. Glancing back to make sure that Jennifer had

not moved and that she and her charge were well

hidden, Rae slid along the tree until she faced the

plain with no cover. Taking a deep breath, she paused,

letting the wind blow into her face to check for any

foreign scents, then she sprinted onto the plain.

Jennifer watched with bated breath, waiting

for her companion to reach the other side. She

gripped Mayline closer as Rae reached the other side

and paused inside the tree line. Nothing moved as

both Racelings waited for anything to reveal itself.

Then Jennifer leaped up, tightened her grip on her

charge, and dashed into the plain. Her breathing

quickened in fear as her feet hit the grass, her long ponytail swinging behind her as she leaped toward the opposite tree line.

Safely on the other side with Rae, Jennifer pressed her back into a tree, panting slightly from the unease that twisted in her stomach. Rae nodded to her, and they both turned to continue their journey to their home.

Moving near silently through the undergrowth, the pair made their way toward a tall tree with a red trunk. The trunk itself was so large, it dwarfed the ones around it. Rae walked up to it and placed her hands against the rough bark. Taking a long, deep breath, she shut her eyes and raised her head. Jennifer shifted and covered her own and Mayline's ears as best as she could.

Rae let out a sharp, piercing howl, raising her voice into the Heavens.

The ground shook, throwing the Racelings to their knees, as the trunk of the tree cracked, and a hidden door opened. Revealing a tall man with golden eyes and silver hair, his face wrinkled with age and kindness. He smiled gently at Rae before glancing worriedly at the still unconscious Mayline. He waved his hands for them to stand and come to him.

"Hurry, girls, we must get her to the infirmary. Is one of you injured? Were you followed?" he asked, helping Jennifer carry Mayline into the hidden room in the tree. Their feet clanged against the metal floor as they entered the confined space inside the tree. Rae grinned up at him.

"No, Mister Harvey. We are alright, and we took care of the Primes that were chasing her," Jennifer said, bracing her back against the wall of the hollow tree. Rae joined her, taking hold of a metal rail that was set into the wall. Harvey pulled the door in the tree closed, and a red light flickered on above

their heads.

"That's good. She escaped herself then? How

much was she injured before you got to her?" he

asked, opening a panel in the wall and pressing a

glowing green button the blinked under a bright red

one. A loud clang sounded, and then the room shifted,

moving downward underground.

"We do not know what happened exactly, but

it's obvious that she was tortured. One of the

Vampires threw her into a tree, and she went

unconscious. Her back feels swollen, and she hasn't

moved since," Jennifer shouted over the sound of the metallic shrieking as the elevator dropped. Harvey's eyes narrowed, and he shook his head.

"She must have been severely injured to not be able to fight back. Mayline is a formidable warrior; she would not have fallen easily," he said, as the elevator began to slow.

As it stopped and the metal doors opened, Harvey took Mayline from Jennifer, his hands feeling the throbbing in her back. Shifting her to a slightly more comfortable position, Harvey nodded his head toward the door.

"You two head to the office. Jordan wanted to speak to you once you were back. I'll take her to the healers," he said and backed out of the elevator, followed by the two women. Jennifer nodded.

"We will go speak with her," she said, taking Rae's arm to start off. Harvey smiled.

"Oh and, girls!" They turned back to look at him. He winked. "Welcome home."

Chapter 4

The Hide

The elevator opened into a large room with a
high ceiling with stone walls holding fluorescent
lights and weapon racks. Racelings milled about,
sharpening swords, gossiping, and eating within the
safety of their hideaway. The walls of the cavern were
jagged rock, stretching high above into the darkness.
Stalactites dripped from the ceiling, puddles of
natural water on the floor beneath them, some caught
by stone and others caught by pails to collect the clear
water. The majority of the floor space was filled by

large tents.

The mess hall, a ragged tent with the opening flaps pinned up, had the only seating directly in front of it in the form of large oak logs cut down into tables. Chairs were a luxury when in hiding. There was little privacy and even less space. The overcrowded cavern teamed with Racelings too afraid of the outside world or too new to their burdened lives to leave the Hide.

Harvey walked with his charge toward a white tent set up in a corner, three women sitting in chairs in front of the entrance. He passed a group of Tracker

Racelings and the men turned and sneered at the

injured girl in his arms.

"Heard she was a Vampire Raceling. Serves

the bitch right," one of them said. Another snorted

and nodded. Harvey's eyes narrowed, and his steps

slowed slightly.

"Any Vampire deserves to die. Attacking other

Racelings… it's just wrong," he grunted.

"Guys, I don't think that's fair. She isn't that

bad. She's pretty nice too!" a young man with black

hair and green eyes said, running his hand through his

hair. His three companions laughed heartily.

"Yeah, right!" one said.

"No Vampire is 'nice,' Josh. Don't be an idiot," said another.

"And do not get too cozy with her either. Or you might start seeing other people start to say the same about you," the tallest one threatened, grabbing the younger male's shoulder roughly.

Harvey paused and turned to the four men. They shifted uncomfortably under his golden stare as he glared at them. He shifted Mayline once again, revealing her burned side to the men watching.

"Mayline Relix has been a Raceling Vampire

for five years now, and she has done more for the Raceling community than you all have in twice that time. She has spent all her time with us, and even before, fighting the tyranny of Chaos and Hellios both. She was captured six days ago while attempting to gather information on Hellios's whereabouts and plans.

"She was coming from the Hall of Cornerstones, attempting to gain the support of the other six Cornerstones to overthrow Chaos. Do not ever, ever, speak such slander about Miss Mayline again, you foolish children. She is more of a warrior than you will ever be," he growled and turned on his heel and continued to the infirmary.

Josh looked at his companions with a smirk, moving away from them to follow Harvey.

"Told you so," he muttered and jogged after the older man.

"Mister Harvey! Sir!" Harvey paused and looked at Josh with a kind smile. Josh grinned up at him as he matched his pace.

"Yes, my boy? How can I help you?" he asked. Josh shrugged and looked at the peaceful face of Mayline.

"I was just wondering… is she going to be alright? She helped me out last week with a mission and… well… she's a really sweet and brave girl…" he said. Harvey smiled down at the younger man.

"She should be just fine. She is just unconscious at the moment. She is strong; she will survive this. She has done so with much worse injuries in the past," he said. Josh smiled, relieved.

"That's good… I was worried when I saw her side. You said she was captured? Did she escape or did someone rescue her?" Harvey huffed slightly and shook his head in mock disbelief.

"Tortured, and malnourished by the looks of it, she escaped but was followed and attacked. From what I gather from the two who brought her in, she put up a brave fight but was outnumbered. Who knows how many she faced before they got the drop on her..." Harvey muttered, eyeing Josh with a twinkle in his eye as they approached the infirmary.

The women took her from Harvey's arms and carried her into the tent before placing her gently on one of the beds.

Josh whistled and shook his head, watching as the Changelings and Banshee worked over the girl.

"She really is one of the best, isn't she?

Trained by Madam Jordan too, right?" he asked.

Harvey nodded, crossing his arms with a sigh.

"Sure was. One of the best to come out of the

Hide in my opinion. Stronger than twelve Demons

and faster than any other Vampire, she is." Harvey

turned and grinned at the boy. "A pretty one too,

wouldn't you say, boy?" Josh blushed slightly and

looked at his feet.

"I… I guess. I mean, I never really noticed,"

he said, rubbing the back of his head with one hand

and shoving his other into the pocket of his navy blue

letterman jacket. Harvey chuckled and patted his shoulder genially.

"I know, son, I was just teasing you. You got more important things on your mind then who is pretty and who isn't. Now, why do not you go and get some food; you look half starved! Mayline will be fine, do not worry. She's in good hands!" Harvey turned and smiled at one of the Changeling nurses. "Isn't that right Macalah?"

A pretty young woman with long black hair and hazel skin smiled at Harvey and nodded. She had a tattoo of an Ankh on her throat and golden bracelets on each wrist. She bowed her head slightly at the

party.

"Yes, sir, she shall be well again in no time, no

time at all!" she assured, her thick Egyptian accent

making it hard to tell what she was saying. Josh

nodded and sighed.

"Yes, sir," he said and turned away, glancing

back over his shoulder at the girl on the bed, her

wounds slowly knitting back together. He walked

back to where the food was being served with a

lighter step now that he knew that Mayline would be

alright.

<u>Chapter 5</u>

The Wrath of Races

Jennifer and Rae walked through the hallway leading to Jordan's office. The carved out hall was well lit by lamps filled with white lights hanging from the rounded ceiling. The two women walked in silence, their footsteps echoing in the cavern. When they reached a wooden door at the end of the hallway, they both paused. The oaken door was thick and heavy looking, but through cracks in the frame, they could see several forms moving around. Jennifer looked down at her companion, and both of them nodded.

Rae knocked on the door lightly.

"Enter," spoke a voice on the other side of the door. The ordinarily soothing tones were harsh and angry. The two women glanced at each other and Rae pushed the door open.

"Ma'am?"

The scene that greeted them was one they had seen many times. Five men and one woman stood around a circular table. The woman had flowing white hair that reached just above her shoulders and bright silver eyes that glared at the men around her with a fire that showed her authority. She was tall with broad

shoulders and muscular arms that flexed as she

crossed them in front of her chest. From her shoulders

sprouted a pair of long, white feathered wings that

curled around her in a protective but menacing way.

Her silver eyes flashed to the two that had entered.

"Yes? What is it?" she asked. Jennifer gulped.

"U-uh, we have retrieved Mayline, Miss

Jordan. She is in the infirmary at the moment." One

of the men scoffed.

"Why even bother? One less Vampire to worry

about says I! Leave her to the Primes!" he growled.

Jordan whirled on him and growled, her wings flaring.

"You watch your words, Jacques! She is one of us, and you will treat her as such!" Another man threw his fist in the air.

"What, like how Chaos and the other Vampiric Racelings treat us? She is no better than the other murderers and traitors! She shouldn't even be here! We should just kill her now and get it over with!" he said, outraged.

Rae snarled at him and leaped on top of the table, her body shaking as her pupils turned into slits in her anger.

"Mayline Relix is ten times the Raceling you

will ever be! She fights every second on both fronts

of the war, and she risked her life to try and get your

Cornerstones to aid us against Chaos! She was

captured by Primes and tortured for days because she

was trying to get information to help your squads in

their upcoming mission! She doesn't follow Chaos's

teachings, and she walks in the footsteps of Peace

himself! How dare you even consider killing off one

of the bravest, kindest, most trustworthy Racelings in

this entire camp, you insolent little worm!" she

shouted, spittle flying from her lips and hitting the

face of the cowering man. Jordan and Jennifer both

blinked at the usually quiet girl. Then Jordan smirked.

"I think, Samuel, that is your cue to step down

from your post as spokesman for the Werewolves,"

she said calmly. Samuel scurried away from the

shaking girl and bolted from the room. Rae turned her

red-tinged eyes to the other man, her teeth bared and

face stormy.

"Anyone else have an opinion against Mayline

Relix? I got tons more where that came from." Her

voice was low, but the threat was obvious.

No one spoke against her, and she slowly

stopped shaking, her eyes returning to their usual bright green. Jordan nodded and turned to Jennifer.

"You said she is in the infirmary. How badly is she injured?" she asked. Jennifer straightened and raised her chin, looking more like a soldier giving her general a report than she should have.

"Her side was burned; her back was swollen; she had several wounds on her arms and legs, and her shoulder had a large stab wound just to the side of her collar bone. She was unconscious when we found her and when we dropped her off at the infirmary. Some of the wounds were as old as two, maybe three, days and some were fresh." Her eyes were fixed on a point straight ahead of her as she spoke, but Jordan could easily see her fists clenching with every wound she recited. The white haired woman sighed and nodded, rubbing her eyes. One man sneered.

"One of my Demons would never have gotten captured in the first place," he said. Rae turned her gaze to him evenly, and he gulped. But it was the door opening without invitation that made everyone pause. Mayline walked in, limping slightly. Her side was bandaged, and her arm was in a sling. She was carrying a scroll in her other hand.

"It's a good thing I was, though, sir. Our contact was in the base where I was held, and I managed to get the needed information from him before I left," Mayline said, tossing the scroll Mortar had given her onto the table. She nodded to Jordan with her eyes downcast, trying not to show the pain of the motion. "I'm afraid there is only one copy of this scroll. Mortar said it was too dangerous to make any more." The Demon man scoffed loudly.

"You know his name? Just shows how sympathetic Vampires are to Prime scum," he said, twisting his mouth into a cruel smile. Mayline glared at him hotly and sneered.

"That Prime scum saved my life and helped me escape from the base, risking himself and his position as our spy to do so. He was kind and talkative and a friend to us to the end. I am proud to know his name. You're unworthy of spitting on his boots if you think he, of all of them, is the scum," she growled. Jennifer beamed at the younger girl.

"You are learning…" she murmured to her. Mayline winked at her. Then Jordan turned to eye the bandages wrapped around Mayline's arms and legs and the garish yellow paste on her torso.

"Shouldn't you be in the infirmary?"

Mayline blanched and looked almost sick.

"Crap…"

The door slammed open, and Macalah stormed in grey eyes.

"Crap, indeed, Miss Relix! This is the last time you are sneaking out while healing, understand?" Macalah barged into the room and took hold of Mayline's ear roughly. She twisted her ear and glared at Mayline.

"You are going right back to that bed, Missy, and I do not want to see you up again until you are completely healed, understand me? Now march!"

"Ow! Macalah, you're going to rip my ear off! Hey! Cut out the pushing! Jennifer, help!" Mayline was pushed out the door, and her protests faded down the hall as Macalah took her back to the infirmary. Jennifer glanced at Rae with a grin as Jordan burst out laughing.

Then Jordan sighed. She turned to face the two girls and held up a sheet of paper.

"Once she is healed up, I have a mission for her. Make sure she gets this, and tell her to pick a team to go with her. She is in no condition for a solo mission." Jordan handed the paper to Jennifer with a heavy look at the younger woman. Jennifer nodded and looked down at the page. Her eyes widened, and she looked back up at Jordan in surprise.

"A Hell Gate? Ma'am, are you sure she is ready for this? You know how she can be when there is a chance of finding... him..." Jordan shook her head.

"No, I'm not sure. Mayline is as stubborn as they come, though. I've already had to deal with her attitude about being passed over for this kind of mission. I think she needs this much more than we know. And if he ends up being there, at least she will have backup."

Jennifer sighed, her shoulders slumping in defeat.

"All right. I will make sure she gets the message."

"Thank you. Now, you both are dismissed. Good night, girls." Jennifer and Rae nodded, turning to leave.

As they stepped through the doorway, the heavy wood swung closed behind them. The two looked at each other and Rae winced slightly.

"You gonna tell her? 'Cause you know she is gonna freak out…" she said. Jennifer nodded and bit her lips in uncertainty.

"Yeah, I'll tell her. But I have no idea how…" She turned and began making her way back into the central area of the Hide.

The infirmary was quiet as Mayline lay awake in the darkness. The other beds were mostly empty, only a few holding injured Racelings. Her blue eyes drifted to the bed beside her where a tiny figure slumbered. The little boy could not have been older than nine years, and yet his body was covered in healing pastes and bandages from battle injuries. His

little chest rose and fell gently, but his face was

scrunched in an uneasy dream. She did not know the

boy personally, only seeing him in passing, but she

knew he was an orphan like her.

Mayline sighed and turned away from the

blond child. She shut her eyes, and the faces of her

torturers flashed in her mind, forcing them open

again. Muttering a curse at her own weakness, she sat

up slowly, careful of her injuries. She swung her legs

over the side of her bed and stood gingerly. She took

a few steps and her back flared in pain. Grunting, she

staggered to the wall of the tent and gripped one of

the support posts. Sighing heavily and wincing as it pulsed down her back, Mayline took hold of one of the spare crutches on the wall. She slowly made her way out of the tent and paused. The cavern was silent and dark, the only light from the elevator and down the hallway to Jordan's office. Several Racelings were sleeping on the floor in various places, even on the tables near the food carts. She sighed.

The Hide had been a place of refuge to all for many generations, but recent Prime activity had created more Racelings with nowhere to go than anticipated. The vast caverns and tunnels that made up most of the Hide were overcrowded on a good day.

They needed a new solution soon, or there wouldn't

be enough food and room for anyone.

Mayline turned from the sleeping Racelings

and looked at the figure slumped in the chair beside

the tent opening. Macalah. The Changeling Raceling

had been kind to Mayline since she had arrived at the

Hide. One of the only ones who looked past her

Vampiric half, Macalah and Mayline had quickly

become fast friends.

As Mayline bent to take one of Macalah's

arms, she grunted in pain and heaved the smaller girl

up and half into her arms. She half carried the

Changeling to the open bed beside her own and laid

her down as gently as she could. Macalah snored

softly as she curled around the small pillow and

Mayline smiled. She threaded her fingers through her

friend's hair and quietly made her way back to bed.

As she laid down again, her eyes drifted shut

despite the images of torture invading her mind. Her

sleep was restless with memories and twisted endings

plaguing her dreams.

Mayline was jolted awake by a hand on her

shoulder. She looked up at the one who had woken

her with a glare only to find two grim-faced women

standing over her cot. Jennifer and a Demoness

Raceling named Rachelle. Mayline and Rachelle had

gone on a few missions together in the past and

become friends, but she had never looked quite so

solemn. Jennifer held up a scroll.

"You have a mission."

Chapter 6

Castle Rock

The sun was just setting, casting thin, broken lines of shadows across the cracked stone floor of the ruins where he stood. Behind him, the large obsidian archway that marked the entrance to Hell stood tall and lonely in the near empty room. The walls of the place were covered in moss and cobwebs, the smell of ancient times clinging to the walls.

He stood at an open window, watching the sunset paint the skies orange, red, and purple, the golden light dancing across his pale skin and giving it a nearly living complexion. His red eyes followed the descent of the sun, marking the time. In the distance, he could see small figures coming closer at a nearly frightening speed. He recognized one of the faces immediately.

"Twilight has come… They should be here soon." His smooth voice slid like cold liquid across the air. He stepped toward the Hell Gate with a smirk upon his thin lips. "Let the games begin."

Out in the fields beyond the stretch of ruins, three young girls halted in their sprinting. Rae and Rachelle glanced at each other as they halted behind their leader.

"Mayline?" Rae asked, reaching toward her friend. Rachelle looked up at the ruined castle they were heading towards and squinted. She gasped and took hold of Rae's arm.

"Rae, look! In the high window, there! Do you see?" Rae squinted up at the window, trying to see the differences in shadows from a distance.

"Movement? I cannot tell what it is-"

"It's him." Both girls looked at Mayline's rigid shoulders. Rae's eyes followed her flexing muscles down to her clenched fists, shaking under the force of

Mayline's squeeze. Mayline ignored the pain in her hands, the venom pooling under her tongue; the roaring in her ears blocked out everything besides the figure standing in the window. "It's Demitri."

Rachelle and Rae glanced at each other then back to the spot where Mayline had been standing a few seconds before. She was already sprinting toward the castle, heedless of the two girls that hesitated to follow her.

They had heard the stories of her change. They felt for their friend and wished her the strength to achieve her revenge. But they had also heard the stories of the general of Hell's armies. Demitri was feared throughout the entire Raceling world; some said even in Hell was he feared and respected. It was this fear that kept them from following Mayline.

Finally, when Rae realized Mayline would go in with or without them, and there were probably more Primes in the ruins than she could handle on her own, she gently hit Rachelle's shoulder with the back of her hand. She nodded toward the ruins and shrugged.

"I'm pretty sure she will need our help in there," she said and started running after the young

Vampire. The Demoness sighed and swallowed her

fear, forcing her feet to start moving.

Mayline's feet pounded across the ground like

war drums, the beating of her heart matching the

thumping of her steps. As she drew near the castle's

entrance, her head started to clear. Her steps slowed

until she was standing just under the open archway

that marked the entrance to the castle. Her chest

heaved, breath coming in quick gasps. Her self

preservation instincts would not let her enter without

backup. But every inch of her body tingled. She could

feel his presence close to her. Just up those stairs…

Her fingers twitched with want to clutch at his throat,

but she held herself back, waiting for the people she

had brought with her for this very reason. As she

heard her friends getting close, Mayline took a single,

small step into the castle.

The setting sun cast no light into the room,

blocked as it was by trees in the distance. Darkness

hung thick in the room, the cloying stench of time

emanating from the floors and walls. But there was

something else… Something moved wraithlike in the

shadows. Scratches echoed in the air; claws scraping

against stone.

In front of her, a strange being about seven

feet tall emerged from the darkness, it's yellow eyes penetrating her very soul. The Werewolf growled, spittle dripping from its angry maw. Mayline took a step back, her hand slipping under her jacket to the dagger laced through her belt. Her fingers curled around the hilt just as the beast opened its jaws and howled. Mayline staggered back as two more wolves came into view. Behind her, Rae and Rachelle ran past her before they noticed the wolves. Rae yelped and dragged the Demoness backward.

"Those are some big-ass dogs…" Rachelle murmured, her eyes becoming wider than Mayline had ever seen them. Rae scoffed.

"I've seen bigger," she said and crouched down. Mayline held up her hand for the two Racelings to pause.

"They are waiting for something," she said, noticing how all three Werewolves stood there, their jowls dripping with saliva. Rae and Rachelle looked at Mayline as she stepped a bit closer. The wolves growled. "Bingo."

Mayline drew her long dagger, sliding her feet apart.

"They're stalling us, and they know we are here to close the gate." Rachelle sneered at the wolves, her eyes turning from her usual green to a stunted orange.

"They're here to open it." Rachelle crouched down and groaned in pain. Mayline turned and watched as the Demoness let out the Demon inside her. Rachelle's skin turned a mottled grey, the ridges of her spinal cord growing larger and sharper. Blood coated the back of her shirt as the bones broke through her skin and tore open the fabric. As she grimaced in pain, Mayline could see her teeth get sharper until the fangs intersected and cut into her lips. Blood bubbled from her mouth, mixing with saliva.

Rachelle opened her eyes. Her pupils were gone - her entire eye was a dark orange. Her fingers started shaking, the bones cutting through the flesh of her fingertips, making bloody claws. The newly transformed Rachelle let out a deep growl, the vibration of the sound shaking the room.

Rae smirked and bent at the waist, forcing her Race side to the front of her mind. The hair all over her body started growing, becoming a blood colored fur. Her green eyes turned yellow; the pupils became slits. Her tailbone broke through her skin, and the skin and hair rushed to cover it, becoming a dog tail. Her ears grew longer and pointed, covered in fur. Her nails grew longer and sharper. The Werewolf growled, bearing the now thick and sharp teeth to her enemies.

Mayline glanced at both her friends with a smirk.

"I'm glad I don't have to change to be a Vampire. That looks painful." Rachelle glared at Mayline and Rae barked out a laugh. The three Racelings looked forward to the Primes before them. Rae growled and launched herself from her crouch and toward the first wolf, closely followed by Rachelle. Mayline leaped toward the wolf on the far left and let out a yell.

The three wolves howled in unison and charged toward them.

Mayline landed just out of reach of the largest wolf, her dagger clenched tightly in her hand and poised to strike. The wolf lunged at her, howling and raising its claws. The giant claws cut into the flesh of her arm as Mayline dodged to the side too slow. She spun around, ignoring the pain, and slashed the dagger across the wolf's flank.

The creature growled and turned to slash at her again. Mayline backflipped out of the way, her palms scraping across the stone floor. As she landed, her foot hit a patch of her own blood and slid out

from under her. She fell to her knees and barely

caught herself with her hands.

"Every time! I swear, every time I try to be

cool and awesome, I fail epically," she muttered as

she tried to stand from the awkward position. The

wolf lunged at her, its jaws open and ready to clench

around her body. Mayline spun to the side and rolled

out of the way, coming up to her feet and leaping to

the side as one of the other wolves flew passed her.

Rachelle chased after the wolf, streaking by in

her low crouch. The Demoness leaped and landed on

the back of the Werewolf, raking her bone claws

across its back and flank. The wolf yelped in pain and

slammed its back into the wall, trapping Rachelle

between its body and the rough stone. Her spinal

bones cracked the wall, sending spider-web lines

across the stone. She looked up as one line reached

the ceiling and smirked as bits of dust, and tiny rocks

fell from the weak point. Rachelle sunk her claws into

the wolf, holding it in place as it tried to run. It

howled in pain as she pierced its flank.

The Demoness looked up again and arched

her back farther into the wall, painfully forcing her

bones into the stone. More cracks appeared,

weakening the ceiling more. Slightly larger pieces started to fall as the lines of cracks went across the ceiling. With one more jerk of her back, a large portion of the ceiling collapsed.

Rachelle pushed off the wall, keeping her claws in the wolf as she vaulted over its back. Her momentum forced the wolf to its knees and into the wall, even as her claws ripped out of its flesh. The giant piece of stone dropped onto the wolf. A pained yelp and then silence. Rachelle grinned, her bloody lips stretching to reveal even more fangs. She turned as she heard a familiar howl. Rae was pinned underneath the last wolf. Rachelle sprinted toward her friend, passing Mayline as she slid under the wolf she

was fighting and slashed its belly open.

Mayline twisted and skidded to a halt as she

watched blood drip from the wolf. The usually

intoxicating smell of blood was tainted by the scent

of hound. The wolf turned toward her, limping

slightly from the wound on its flank. It shook slightly,

either from pain or anger Mayline wasn't sure.

Suddenly, the creature collapsed, shaking so badly it

was nearly vibrating.

Mayline stood in confusion, watching the fur

recede slightly. She blinked and cursed as the wolf

started healing as it went into its human form. She

started running forward, but the woman was already

standing up. She turned, and Mayline skidded to a

halt. Her face was still wolflike, but her body was

human. As she turned fully toward the Raceling,

Mayline noticed the fur still covering where she had

cut across the belly. The Werewolf had healed herself,

but where the fur was still on her body, she was still

healing. Mayline dropped back into a crouch.

Rae struggled under the bigger wolf, her tail

trapped beneath its back paw. She could feel its hot

breath at her neck, ready to bite through her bones.

She tried to think of a way out, but her mind wasn't

working right. She was well and truly trapped and royally screwed.

The wolf on top of her reared back, preparing to strike. Rae closed her eyes and sent a silent prayer for salvation, from the wolf, death, or Hell she did not really care. Her prayer was answered with a deep roar. Rachelle pounced on the wolf, dragging it off of her friend. Rae rolled away and pulled herself up off the ground, looking at the Demoness on top of the wolf that almost killed her. Rachelle leaped off and landed beside Rae.

"You alright, mutt?" Rachelle asked. Rae

grinned and nodded.

"Thanks, Lizard," she said. Rachelle chuckled darkly as the wolf in front of them stood slowly and shook itself, glaring and bearing its teeth at them.

"Ready to mess 'em up, Little Red?" the Demoness asked. Rae dropped into a crouch and cracked her knuckles.

"Bring it." The Prime charged.

Chapter 7

The Ephemeral Prime

Mayline and the Werewolf woman circled each other slowly, both wary of the other. Mayline let her eyes dart over the woman's body, taking in her stance and possible weak points in her defenses. Her gaze zeroed in on the woman's left hand. It was slightly lower than the other, farther out with a slight bend and left her left side was wide open. Mayline looked back up at her opponent's yellow eyes in time to see them fade to brown and back to yellow.

Mayline glanced at the door they had come through.

The sun had set, and the moon was rising through a window to her right. It was no longer full. There was her opening.

Mayline charged forward, striking to the right. The woman moved to block, but Mayline fainted away and struck across the left side, slicing through the woman's ribs and up to her chest. She howled and fell back, holding her bleeding side with her right hand and keeping her left raised to defend. Mayline leaped, her unnatural strength sending her far above the Werewolf's head. She raised her dagger and flipped midair, sending her foot outward. Her heel hit the woman's left arm away as Mayline brought her blade down toward the woman's neck. The edge cut

through the flesh like butter, going down across the

woman's collarbone and across her breast. The

Werewolf howled, her body turning fully human as

she fell onto her back. Her skin was a dark brown

with black hair cropped up to her chin. Mayline

looked down at the Middle Eastern woman with a

cold stare. She stared up at Mayline fearfully with her

dark brown eyes.

"Are you going to kill me, Bloodling?" she

asked. Her voice was scared but steady. Mayline

tilted her head and stared down at the woman whose

life she held in her hand, pondering the worth of her

life.

Mayline wasn't fond of killing. She spared

lives whenever she could, even Primes. The only

death she had ever wanted on her hands was

Demitri's. But this wasn't a time where it was

practical to spare a life. One wolf had already died in

that castle, the question was, would this one?

"What is your name?" she asked, dropping her

knife to rest on the unmarred side of the woman's

neck.

"Sehar," she said through her teeth. Mayline

nodded as she knelt beside the wolf.

"Sehar, I am going to let you live, but I will not let you go unharmed. Nor, will I let you go just for you to come after us as we move up this building." Relief seemed to shake through Sehar's body, but she steadily watched the girl with a knife at her throat.

"So what will you do with me?" Sehar asked, glaring.

Mayline thought about it. She could feel the blood rage that came with a fight, the hunger for the blood pouring from the wounded, the anger and hate that came from being near a natural enemy… For once, she let the Race in her take over.

"I said I wouldn't kill you. I never said anything about my friends." Sehar's eyes widened and her head whipped around to look at the Racelings fighting the last of the wolves.

Rachelle dodged to the side as the wolf she was fighting pounced at her. Rae leaped up to land on its back. She sunk her claws into its neck as Rachelle lunged forward and slid under the wolf, using both hands full of bone claws to shred the wolf's underbelly. Rae ripped her claws up toward her body, lacerating the throat of the wolf.

The two Racelings jumped away, Rae flipping in the air and landing in a crouch as Rachelle skidded and spun around. The wolf was standing still for a few seconds before it fell to its side, its insides spilling out onto the stone and its head separated from its body. The two girls looked back at Mayline and Sehar.

Sehar's breathing was ragged with fear as all three Racelings closed in around her.

"This is Sehar," Mayline said, standing straight. "I won't kill her." Rae and Rachelle looked at Mayline knowingly. Rachelle turned and snarled at their captive.

"Dibs," she muttered.

"Wait!" Sehar yelled, holding up her hands. "I can help you! We were not the only ones here!" Rae rolled her eyes.

"We already know there is someone at the top."

"But you do not know who is between you and the gate," Sehar said, coughing slightly as the wound in her neck started leaking blood into her throat. Rachelle sneered and raised her bone claws at the wolf.

"I think I will slice her up and feed on her flesh. She smells quite appetizing…" she said. Mayline did not even blink at her friend's brutality.

"No, please! I'll tell you anything you want to know! Please, do not kill me!" Sehar was nearly crying in fear. Rae scoffed and crossed her arms.

"Primes are such cowards. Their longevity makes them fear mortality," she said, her voice dripping disdain. Mayline nodded.

"It's almost pathetic how much they plead for their lives. Their pride is so high when they view us as lesser for our humanity, but once they are defeated their superiority complex fails them." Sehar gulped

but did not rise to the bait. Mayline knelt beside her

and fingered her bloody dagger.

"What can you tell us of what lies in wait,

little Sehar?" she asked. Sehar glanced from Rachelle

to Mayline and shook her head.

"There are other Primes on each level. Angels,

Demons, Banshees, Changelings... They all wait for

you up those stairs," Sehar said, unable to keep in her

arrogant tone. Mayline raised an eyebrow.

"It would seem as though we have been issued

a challenge, my friends. Perhaps we should send these

Primes a message," she said and stood slowly.

"Rachelle." The Demoness smiled coldly, her large

teeth cutting into her lips more. Sehar shook her head.

"No-No! Please!"

Mayline turned away, trying not to care about

the death of yet another enemy. The sound of ripping

flesh filled the air as she started toward the stairs.

Mayline tried to block out the screams from Sehar,

but every instinct she had in her humanity told her to

stop the killing.

A Vampire who would not kill… Chaos would

be so disappointed in her if he took the time to care

about her existence. She brought her hand to rest on

the rail of the stairs, the metal nearly crumbling under

her touch, and looked back.

Rachelle, still in Demon form, stood over the

mutilated body of Sehar. Rae stood halfway between

Mayline and Rachelle, her furry hide matted with

blood. The two girls turned to look at Mayline, even

as Rachelle's claws dripped with blood. The Vampire

tried to hold in her gag, but she ended up making a

face.

"Let's just get the rest of this over with," she

sighed. Rachelle had the decency to look at her kill

with a slightly apologetic look before following her

two friends up the stairs.

Chapter 8

Savagery of the Cursed

Mayline paused just before they would have been visible. If Sehar had told the truth, more enemies awaited them on the next floor. Would it be wise to just barge in? She held a hand for her companions to wait.

Mayline raised her head, trying to sense what was waiting for them. She shut her eyes, using her other senses. The smell of blood lingered in the air, wolf, Demon, something else… Something almost too faint… Mayline's eyes snapped open.

"Banshees," she hissed, barely audible. Rae

tensed and scowled. Banshees were the mothers of

many different Races, including Werewolves. Rae's

own change happened at the hands of a vindictive

Banshee. Though the Enchantment was never

completed, giving her the status of Raceling, she still

harbored the natural hatred that came from being

cursed.

Mayline knew they could not just barge up the

stairs, metaphorical guns blazing. Banshees might not

have as good of hearing as Vampires or Werewolves,

but the fight had made enough noise to be noticed by

even the most unobservant human. The Banshees

would be expecting them. But would they be

expecting them to know they are up there? Sehar had

warned them, but did the Banshees hear that?

Mayline lifted her hand, murmuring for her

friends to wait on her. She slowly stepped up to the

next step, ducking her head but raising her eyes. She

tried to distinguish the shadows - tried to count them.

She squinted. Was that three? Four? No... Shadows

did not move that way in the amount of light in the

room. Three. She raised her hand, splitting her fingers

to tell Rae and Rachelle there were three waiting for

them. The wolf and Demoness shared a look.

Mayline bit her lip, trying to come up with a way to attack without getting killed. Banshees may not be the most powerful of the Races, but they were one of the smartest. The creatures would be lying in wait for them to rush up. There was probably a spell ready to be thrown aimed right for the top of the stairs. Mayline smirked. Banshees were known for their hair triggers when casting spells.

Mayline untied her belt, knotting it up until it was a suitable size ball. She glanced behind her and nodded to her friends. The girls prepared themselves to rush up the remaining stairs as Mayline turned back and pulled her arm backward. Then she threw the ball in her hand straight up the stairs. Three

flashes of light incinerated the belt as the three

Racelings sprinted up the stairs. Mayline twisted mid-

stride, flipping sideways to avoid running into a

metal, decaying lampstand and shot her hand out to

catch her extra weight. Rae leaped over her, eyes feral

as she howled and galloped toward the nearest

undead sorceress. Mayline stood and raised her knife

to deflect a cutting spell as Rachelle dug her claws

into the stone wall, using them to climb the walls like

a spider.

One of the Banshees hissed and started

levitating towards Rachelle. The sorceress flung her

hand out toward the Demoness, a ball of green light

shooting from her fingertips as ancient words dropped

from her tongue. Rachelle swung with her claws in

the ceiling to dodge the spell. The Banshee opened

her mouth and spit out a jet of green flames. Rachelle

shouted in pain as she dodged too slow and the fire

hit her shoulder. Her feet hit the ceiling again, and she

ripped her claws from the stone, twisting to fall

straight toward the coming Banshee, her claws

stretching toward the sorceress.

A metallic screech filled the air as Rachelle's

unholy claws ripped through the spirit woman, cutting

her body into shreds. Rachelle hit the ground and

looked back. The fragments of the woman hung in midair before they began stitching themselves back together. Rachelle cursed and looked toward Mayline who was locked in close combat with another Banshee, dodging the curved blade the sorceress swung at her.

"Mayline! They are immune to my claws!" Rachelle roared, dodging another green spell and holding the burn on her shoulder. Mayline grunted as she blocked a particularly hard blow to her side with her much smaller dagger.

"I noticed!" she yelled back, eyeing the healed

wounds she had given her own opponent. A loud bark filled the air, and Mayline looked toward the third party of their group.

Rae had leaped toward the wall behind the Banshee she was fighting, hitting the stone and turning to go for the unprotected back of the sorceress. The Banshee cried out in fear as the Werewolf's claws sank into her now corporeal flesh. Rae flipped over the woman's head, twisting one hand to her neck. She landed and rolled to the right, immediately going for the Banshee's side. Her teeth cut through the fabric of the sorceress's dress and into her arm, ripping it off from the elbow. Rae was heedless of the screams from her opponent, her

yellow eyes seeing nothing but red. The Banshee fell

to her knees, clutching at her missing arm. Rae

twisted and grabbed a handful of the Banshee's long

blond hair. She put a clawed foot onto the sorceress's

back and growled, ripping her hand backward while

pushing as hard as she could with her foot.

The Banshee's head came off, her body falling

forward under the force of Rae's foot. Rae held up the

head of her enemy and let out a long, triumphant

howl.

The remaining Banshees looked over and

stared in shock alongside the Racelings. Rae growled,

staring at the remaining sorceresses. The one closest

to Rachelle gulped and raised her hand to fire off a

spell. It was as if something snapped. Rae sprinted

forward, blocking the spell with the head still in her

hand. Her image seemed to blur with her speed as she

threw the now smoking head at the Banshee and

leaped over her. The woman screamed as she held the

head of her sister sorceress even as Rae ripped the

ancient lampstand from its spot in the stone. She

leaped onto the wall, tossing the lamp up and kicking

it.

The Banshee turned just as the metal came

flying toward her, impaling her through the chest. The

end of the lamp went through the wall opposite Rae,

pinning the dead Banshee between the wall and the

ball of glass where a candle once sat. The remaining

Banshee turned and tried to run to the stairs, but Rae

cut her off by leaping from the wall, leaving holes

where her claws had dug into the stone. She landed

just in front of the stairway and turned to growl at the

sorceress.

The terrified woman turned to run up the other

stairs, but Rachelle and Mayline were there, looking

on with nearly detached interest. The Banshee

hesitated, but that was all Rae needed. The Werewolf

rushed forward and jerked her arm forward.

Mayline watched as Rae's blood-covered hand appeared through the Banshee's chest, clutching at a blackened heart. The Banshee slumped and fell as Rae ripped her arm back out of the body. Rachelle and Mayline stared at their friend, astonished at her feats.

Rae's tense body slowly relaxed as her fevered brain registered that all of the Banshees were dead. She blinked, her vision returning to normal. Rae glanced down at her bloody hand, still holding the heart. She growled at the dying organ and opened her hand lazily, allowing it to drop to the floor and land with a squelch. She looked up at her friends and sniffed slightly, rubbing a bloody hand over her snout.

"Banshees can only be killed by a Race they Sired," she explained, shrugging slightly, almost embarrassed. "Otherwise they just come back…" Rachelle grinned and shook her head in wonder.

"I knew we brought you along for a reason, mutt!" she said with a laugh. Rae sent her friend a mock glare.

"Keep laughing, Lizard, one of these floors has Angels!" Rae said, and Rachelle's grey skinned face seemed to pale.

"Oh, yeah… Shit." The Demoness heaved a sigh and looked over at Mayline. The Vampire was staring at the bodies of the Banshees, looking green.

"Mayline?" Rae asked worriedly. Mayline's hand flew to her lips.

"I think I'm gonna be sick…" she murmured and screwed her eyes shut, turning away from the carnage. Rae looked around at the death she had caused and then back to her friend, shamefaced and upset.

"May, I…" she started, but the words died in

her throat as Mayline shook her head. The Vampiress

began walking toward the next set of stairs, not able

to look back.

Rachelle watched the exchange with sad eyes.

Though the Demon inside her was ecstatic at the

bloodshed, her humanity was saddened at her friend's

plight. A Raceling who despised death as much as

Mayline should not have had to deal with it as much

as she did. But Rachelle and Rae both knew that

Mayline would rather die than allow others to be hurt

the way she and her family had been.

The two turned to follow her up the stairs,

both now covered in their enemies' blood. The steps

were covered in a layer of dust, with footprints

pressed into the surface. Mayline paused, counting the

sets. A large pair and a smaller pair. She looked up at

the next floor and sighed. Three more deaths on her

hands that day. She sniffed the air and for the first

time since her change the lingering scent of blood

turned her stomach. She could smell sulfur, stronger

in front of her than behind her where Rachelle stood,

and the scent of rotten bone marrow. The heavy

metallic scent hung thick in the air as pungent as

fettered blood.

Her eyes snapped open, and she hissed.

"Demon and possibly Changeling. We need to move fast. Prime Changelings shift faster than Racelings," she said. Rachelle crooked a claw at the other two girls and smirked, her bleeding lips making the expression grotesque.

"Demons have a very special weakness, ladies. We have bad backs," she said, gesturing to the bones sticking out of her back. Mayline smirked and raised an eyebrow.

"So your bones grow to protect the weaker area. Interesting. What do we know of Changelings, then? Weaknesses?" Rae coughed, still upset about losing control.

"Well, I know that with blood they can change to any form they desire, but also if they are old enough, they can use two forms at once. And shift certain parts of their bodies only." Mayline grimaced and nodded.

"Let's pray to the Creator that we have a young one on our hands. Now, let's move. We need to work quickly now. Who knows if Demitri has already opened the gate or not," she said and turned back to the stairs. Rachelle and Rae followed her as she stepped up onto the staircase. Mayline took a deep breath…

And sprinted straight up the stairs.

Chapter 9

The Price of Prime

Mayline's eyes scanned around her faster than humanly possible. She dodged to the side as a stone was sent flying toward her head. It broke across the wall behind her, showering the steps with smaller stones, nearly hitting Rachelle's face. Rachelle crouched and leaped to the wall then bounced off of it and toward the Demon that was rushing toward Rae. The Werewolf ducked as the two Demons collided with a force that shook the stones. Mayline sprinted toward the woman in the corner, her knife raised. The woman was leaning against the wall, seemingly unaware of the coming Raceling. Mayline narrowed

her eyes and slowed to a stop before reaching her. The

Changeling smirked, standing straight. Mayline

snarled, warning the Prime to stay back. The woman

merely laughed and crouched deeply.

"So you are the little pest Demitri warned us

of. You do not look like much. You're not even a

hatchling yet!" the Changeling cackled, her heavy

accent familiar to Mayline. Louisiana Cajun. The

woman raised her hand and grinned darkly. In her

palm rested a small glass tube of blood. Mayline

snarled. She could smell the fresh blood, but she

couldn't make out the creature. The woman popped

the cork off the bottle with her thumb and raised it to

her lips, quickly downing the liquid and swallowing.

She tossed the bottle away, shattering across the floor,

as her skin began to steam. Mayline took a step back

but was quickly knocked forward by a flying

Werewolf. The two Racelings fought to disentangle

themselves from the other, both arguing loudly.

"Rae! Get your fat dog butt off my hip!"

Mayline yelled angrily, trying to push her friend off

of her lower body.

"It's not my fault! That bastard Demon kicked

me!" Rae cried back, trying to maneuver off of

Mayline with their legs tangled together.

"Well then kick him back!" Mayline twisted to get free, clawing at the stone under her. Rae was pulled back slightly with Mayline's motion, and she huffed loudly.

"You're stupid bloodsucking ass needs to get off me first!"

"Would both of you idiots shut up and help me kick this guy's ass, please!" Rachelle yelled to the both of them as she ducked a swipe from her opponent.

Rae and Mayline looked over to where

Rachelle and the Demon were struggling with each other. Rachelle's spinal protection was much thinner and shorter than the man's, marking her as a younger and therefore weaker Demon. The older Hellspawn was taking advantage of this, easily snapping pieces of her spine off. Mayline growled and kicked Rae off of her legs and flipped to her feet, skidding slightly. She quickly jumped over Rae and rolled, stopping beside Rachelle with one leg out and the other bent. She lifted her dagger and growled.

Rae scrambled to her feet, facing the Changeling who looked slightly put out that her prey had gone to another. Rae grinned and lifted her hands as she shrugged.

"You don't mind the switch do you?" she asked, and the Changeling snarled, the steam becoming a cloud around her. It seemed to happen too quickly for Rae to see, even with her Raceling eyes. The woman's skin became scales. She fell to her knees as her limbs became shorter and her face became longer.

A low hiss filled the air and Rae took a step back. Rae yelped as a fifteen-foot-long alligator sprung out of the steam and launched itself at her. Rae quickly tried to dodge, but the gator swung its tail around and caught her in the side, sending her flying into the wall. She hit the stone hard, cracking some of the wall where her shoulder hit. She grunted, slowly trying to pick herself up from her stunned state.

She froze at the long hiss. The jaws of the gator were right in front of her, the smell of rotted flesh heavy. Hot breath blew her fur back, forcing her to blink against the drying air in her eyes. The wolf cringed as she tried to slowly back away, but the gator struck. The wolf tried to move away but was too slow. The jaws latched onto her arm, and Rae screamed.

The wolf howled and swung her free arm

around, her claws scraping across the Changeling's

eye. The gator let go and reared back, hissing. Rae

smirked, despite the intense pain in her arm. She

knew that never would have made a real alligator let

go, but the Prime had the instincts of a human when it

came to self-preservation. The wolf rolled away,

clutching a hand to her injured arm and baring her

teeth at the Changeling. The gator hissed loudly and

turned to lunge at Rae again, but she was too slow.

Rae leaped over the Changeling's back and

flipped midair to slow down enough to not go passed

her prey. Blood droplets flew through the air as Rae

brought both her feet down onto the gator, cracking

its spine. The Changeling roared, pain forcing her to shift back to her human form. She lay there on the stone floor, gasping but not moving. Rae stepped away from her and turned to her friends' battle.

"Wait! Do not leave me here like this! Kill me please!" she said. Rae turned back to her, raising an eyebrow.

"You could heal from that wound. Why give up your life?" Rae asked. The Changeling grunted as she tried to move her head, but the ability was beyond her with her injured spine.

"If I live, I will be punished for letting you get

away! For being defeated by mere Racelings would forfeit my life anyway. Please! Kill me now and spare me the torture by my master's hand!" she said, voice broken by pain. Rae looked down at her opponent with cold eyes.

"Tell me one thing before I do slay you," she said.

"Anything!"

"If you were shown another way of living, outside of Hellios's insanity and fighting and war, would you leave Hell for it? If it were peaceful, all Races working together as one for the survival of all?

Racelings and Primes alike?" Rae asked. The

Changeling snarled.

"A life outside of war is a life of fairy tales!

Hellios will control all things!" Rae sighed and

nodded her head.

"I would have offered to take you with us

when we go home to protect you from Hellios, but

now… I grant your wish." The Changeling's eyes

widened as Rae raised her claws.

"Wait- no! I didn't know there was another

option! No! Please! No-"

Her begging was cut off by gurgling as Rae's

claws sank into the Changeling's throat.

Mayline twisted over the Demon's head and slashed down toward his neck, her dagger clipping his spinal bone as he tried to dodge. Rachelle lunged toward his side, knocking him to the ground as Mayline landed again. She dove forward and shoved her dagger toward his throat, but he rolled away, trapping Rachelle underneath him. Another of her spinal bones snapped, but she ignored the pain to kick him off of her and roll to the side as Mayline jumped over her. Mayline landed on her hands and rolled toward the Demon as he stood and turned to them. He froze, Mayline's dagger piercing his stomach, curving up to tickle his heart.

"I have just punctured your diaphragm, a major artery, and I am inches away from your heart. You have approximately three minutes until you choke on your own blood, Demon. I suggest you make them count. Apart from Demitri, how many are up there waiting for us?" Mayline asked, her voice deceptively calm. The Demon coughed, his orange eyes were wide. He slowly curled his fingers at his side. Rachelle watched them since Mayline was focused entirely on her opponent.

"Two. Two are up there waiting for us," she

said. Mayline nodded.

"Thank you for your assistance, Demon. May the Creator show mercy on your soul," she said and pushed the final few inches to pierce the heart. As she pulled away, the lifeless body dropped from her blade. Rae came to join the others as Mayline stood straight.

"You killed him? But I thought-" Rae was cut off by Mayline turning away from the body and spilling the contents of her stomach onto the ground. Rachelle gagged and turned away, Rae making a disgusted but sympathetic face.

"Mayline…" Rachelle murmured. Rae put a hand on Mayline's back, trying to comfort her. The Vampiress waved the pair off, wiping her lips with the back of her hand and wiping her hand on her jeans.

"Forget about my inability to properly kill something without throwing up, and let's get upstairs. Demitri is waiting for me."

When Mayline raised her head, her eyes were completely red, not a hint of blue left in the usually bright and welcoming orbs. She licked her teeth, the edges of which slowly became sharper until not just her fangs were lethal, but her entire mouth resembled a shark's.

"I'm ready to end this once and for all," she said.

Their feet barely made any noise as they ascended the final set of stairs. There was no talking, no jesting, no planning… They all knew what the plan was. Rachelle and Rae would hold off the two extras while Mayline went for Demitri's throat. Once all enemies were neutralized or escaped, as Rae personally believed Demitri would end up as, then the Hell Gate was to be closed and destroyed. Of course, nothing ever goes according to plan, as the trio had come to learn. As they came to the last step, Rachelle

glanced around the room, taking in the emptiness.

In front of her was an empty stone room with

only a window facing the last colors of the sunset. In

the back left corner was the Hell Gate. It was a

hulking mass of black jet and obsidian shaped like a

rectangular doorway. The top of the frame was held

by pillars ending in claws grasping the edges. From

the bottom of the frame sprung blue flames that cast

no light. Tentacles of flesh hung from the top, draping

like beads over the doorway. They writhed.

Confusion bled into Rachelle's features. The

Hell Gate was indeed open, but there didn't seem to be anything else in the room. She looked around, trying to find any signs of spellcraft or anything hiding. She saw nothing, but her skin still crawled.

"Guys? There's no one here," she said.

"What?!" Mayline pushed passed the Demoness and the Werewolf and into the center of the room, setting off a chain reaction. Rae tried to grab her, calling for her to wait, and Rachelle stumbled back into something fleshy that burned her skin. Two Angels materialized out of nowhere, one wrapped his arms around Rachelle from where he was with her leaning against him and the other swooped down to

tackle Rae from behind. Mayline was forced to her

knees by the weight of a large body dropping from the

ceiling. A man with long, dark black hair pulled into a

loose ponytail quickly stepped off of Mayline but

kept a foot on her long brown hair. The man wore a

black, long sleeved button up shirt with all but the

bottom three buttons open, coupled with pitch black

trousers and silver studded belt. His skin was milky

white apart from around his crimson eyes were there

appeared to be bruising. His thin lips parted to show

his own shark-like teeth. He bent slowly, trailing an

abnormally sharp nail down Mayline's cheek.

"We meet again, at last, my darling Mayline. Oh, I have missed you so... How sweet of you to finally come and find me. I was afraid you would hide away forever, and I'd never get to finish what I started five years ago!" he said, his voice mockingly pleasant. Rae struggled against her captor's hold on her, barking menacingly.

"Get away from her!"

"Don't touch her, you bastard!" Rachelle joined in, despite the pain from being held by an Angel. The man turned and grinned at the girls.

"And you brought friends? How sweet,"

Mayline growled her hand curling around the man's

ankle, claws digging into his hard skin.

"Demitri." The man smiled brightly.

"Mayline. Oh, that reminds me!" he looked up

at Rachelle and Rae.

"You're all here to close my Hell Gate, aren't

you? Well, sorry girls, but I've already opened it! It

can still be closed of course, but really, this was all

just a set up to get you here. More specifically," he

looked back at Mayline, smile gone and all pretenses

of pleasantries dropped.

"To get you here, my dear. You see, my master

has taken such an interest in you that he went to the

bunker where you were being held! But - naughty girl

- you ran away before he could meet you. So it's up to

me to get you two together now. Such a shame too…"

Demitri knelt to her level, his lips brushing Mayline's

ear.

"I was so looking forward to killing you

myself," Demitri said with a smile.

Despite her situation, Mayline could not help

feeling at home with Demitri's close proximity. She

shivered from the feeling, disgusted with her apparent

comfort around her Sire. Demitri closed his eyes,

fighting the same feeling but also enjoying breathing in her scent once again after so long. He had not lied when he had said he'd missed her. The girl had never once been far from his thoughts. The delicious meal and lovely possible bed warmer that had got away… But now, he had a job to do. No matter how distasteful it was to him.

Demitri stood with that thought, removing his foot from Mayline's hair. He instead grabbed a fistful of her brown mane and dragged her painfully to her feet. He turned her to face the Hell Gate, a jet stone archway filled with a molten red and orange light.

"And now, little one, I do believe it is time for you to meet your maker's master!" he said and flung Mayline around him by her hair in an arch, letting her fly into the portal. Rachelle roared and struggled against her captor. Rae screamed shrilly.

Mayline was gone.

Chapter 10

Hell's Welcome Mat

Mayline turned around quickly, her heart

pounding in fear. The portal behind her closed. She

was trapped inside the pits of Hell. Alone.

She had to find a way out; she had things to

finish, fights to win… the blood of her Sire to spill.

Her fists clenched with resolve. She would

find a way out. Even Hell was escapable for those not

meant to be there. That thought made Mayline pause.

Did she belong there? In the flames and the sulfur and

the torture? Did she really have the right to escape?

She was half Vampire; half murderer… Half monster.

Her Race had been born of the Balanie, a Hell dragon,

so why did she believe her slight humanity gave her

the right to salvation? Should she even try?

Despair seemed to overtake her other

emotions, a black pit in her mind. There was no point

in trying to achieve salvation when she was already

damned.

The air around her smelled of sulfur and

blood, rotting flesh and burning hair. The screams of

the damned were so loud, even distant as she was

from the rings of torture, they were the only thing she

could hear. Her hands clenched at her hair of their

own accord, trying to block out the sounds, the calling

for a reprieve.

Mayline shut her eyes and her own voice

mixed with the screaming souls. Her tears sizzled

against the boiling flesh beneath her feet.

Madness and torture went hand in hand, but

now Mayline knew which one came first. She

dropped to her knees, the squelch of the fleshy floor

lost as her screaming and crying rose in volume.

Mayline's mind seemed to darken under a fog of

despair and pain, betrayal from the friends who had promised they would protect her. The anger at the Racelings for not saving her family- Family...?

Her family had taught her well that salvation was not withheld from anyone. Salvation was a breath away even at that moment. Mayline's eyes snapped open, and her voice rose again, but her screams were not of pain but desperation.

"Creator in Heaven, I beg You, free my mind from this place's power. Break the chains upon my heart. I pray to You from the pit. Please! Open my eyes beyond this darkness and hate. Creator, I pray

You will guide my heart back to the light. Creator of all things, lift my soul from despair! Savior, give me the strength to fight this Hell."

She may not have realized how far her voice carried; for, over a mound of rotting flesh and bone that seemed to move with breath, two heads popped up to listen to her prayer. The creatures were not human or even humanoid, not recognizable as Demon nor Hellspawn. These creatures were short, stubby, walking on four legs with wings that seemed too shredded to fly.

They crawled out of the mound of flesh and

what appeared to be pieces of the pile stuck to them

were actually their own skin. Their eyes were black

holes in their heads, noses merely slits, but the

mouths were small and lipless with tiny fangs jutting

out from the maw. Their ears, long and pointed with

slashes through them, burned at the mention of the

Creator's names, but neither one turned away. Souls

who were trapped in Hell did tend to pray for

salvation, but always for deliverance from the pit

itself and never just from its effects. The larger of the

two creatures looked to the other and then they were

flying on their shredded wings, carrying the message

that a soul was not completely lost.

Mayline panted, the weight of her breaths leaving trails of steam in the air. It was so hot that her lukewarm breath was colder than the air, a reverse chill effect. Mayline shook her head, squinting.

'I don't have time for this. I need to find a way out of here. Creator willing...' she thought, her hands coming out of her hair at last. She sat up slightly and looked around her. The red, engorged landscape opened up into a canyon that seemed to stretch farther than even her eyes could see. She slowly stood up fully and wiped a hand across her eyes. She took a deep breath that was filled with fetid scents and let it out slowly.

"Alright," she said, her eyes slowly filling with resolve. "Let's do this."

"Not so fast, Bloodling." Mayline spun around, and her eyes went wide as the net was tossed over her. The cords were woven together burned against her skin, leaving red welts wherever they touched her. She cried out in pain and dropped back to the ground, her hands trying to push the net aside but to no avail.

"Sorry, kid. Looks like Master Hellios will get his new toy after all. Blane! Grab her and take her to the throne room!" Mayline's vision grew blurry as a shadowed figure stepped into her line of sight. The

pain from the burning net forced her eyes shut, her

body finally becoming too weak to continue. The

stress of her torture and escape plus the pain from her

new wounds and the fear of being alone in Hell

forced her body into an unnatural shutdown. As she

slowly lost consciousness, she could feel the figure's

hands clenching around the net and bringing her up

over his shoulder. Her head lolled to the side as her

clouded vision turned black.

Mayline's eyes slowly opened, squinting

against the bright light of the fires around her as she

slowly came back into consciousness. The room

around her was hot, warmed as it was by the bonfires

dotted throughout the cavern-like room. The ground

beneath her for the first time since she arrived in Hell

was solid and dry, cold stone pressing into her palms

as she attempted to rise. A sickening thud echoed in

the room as a hard piece of metal struck Mayline in

the back of the head. Her vision blurred and darkened

again as she dropped back to the ground, her cheek

scraping against the stone. She coughed, blood thick

as oil splashing across the rocks in front of her.

"Now, now, Blane, let's at least let our guest

stand." A thick, dark-coated voice rasped from somewhere in the room. Mayline's eyes, vision still dark, shifted to look around the room, searching for the owner of the deliciously dangerous voice. Boots filled the area she could see, the steel toes pausing to tilt her chin up slightly.

"Stand up, bitch. Our master wishes to speak with you." The cold tones of this voice were unsettling. They spoke of cruelty and the torture that was most certainly in her future. Mayline grit her teeth.

Today just wasn't her day.

Pressing her palms to the pavement once more, she pushed herself to her knees. Her left knee hit a protruding rock, cutting the skin ever so slightly. Blood began to dribble out even as the small wound sealed itself as her venom oozed through the cut and knit the skin together. Mayline slowly got to her feet, ignoring the blood in the corner of her mouth. Her eyes drifted over the man with the steel-toed boots, meeting his amber gaze and returning his arrogant stare with one of defiance.

Mayline twisted her lips into a snarl, her blue eyes bleeding into burgundy. The man before her grinned, his teeth white as bleached bones and small rivulets of venom rolling down his teeth as the glands

secreted the liquid at the sight of his supposed prey.

Mayline had no intentions of being tortured for the

second time in as many days. She eyed the man,

searching for weaknesses. She found none. Turning

now to face in front of her, Mayline's slow pulsing

heart froze. Fear crept through her body like ice,

forcing blood to stop, her limbs to go numb, her

breath to catch in her throat, her mouth to hang

uselessly…. Before her stood the man of her

nightmares, the one she had feared since the day she

was told what she had been forced to become.

"Welcome to Hell, my dear little Relix. Oh,

the stories I have heard of you from my friends have kept me on edge just waiting to meet you!"

The dread that filled Mayline's heart at those words nearly brought her to her knees.

The man before her, swathed in black robes fixed with a golden cord around his waist with a silver crown resting upon his heavily styled auburn hair and gold feathered wings folded over the back of the throne, not only knew of her but had plans for her. His cold, silver eyes bore into her as he approached from the black throne he had risen from. His smile was translucent, showing right through the façade of pleasantries to the core of his hatred.

The fires that lit his eyes burned through Mayline, igniting inside her belly her own fever of hatred and melting the ice that had paralyzed her body. Her teeth clenched, lips pulling back to bare the white bones to her enemy, her hands turning claw-like as she dropped into a low crouch. A deep, bass growl built within her chest, rumbling through her throat to be released as a massive roar that shook the stones beneath her feet. Her powerful legs forced her body forward as she pounced toward her enemy.

"Die, you bastard!"

The man before her sidestepped, slamming a steady hand into the back of her head and sending Mayline's face straight into the ground once again. A sickening crunch followed by spurts of blood signified the break of her nose.

Mayline gasped in pain, eyes tearing up slightly before she could blink them away. She struggled back to her feet, blood pouring down her face. The pain of the break was quick, but the slow healing and cracking as the cartilage was forced back into place by her venomous healing was much more painful. She turned to face Hellios once again, ready to attack again. He sighed softly and tutted at her as he moved back to his jet stone throne.

"My, my, such a temper on her. No wonder our Demitri was so entranced by you when he first found you and tasted of your blood." Hellios laughed, and Blane joined in hesitantly. Mayline growled again, her frustration finally winning out over her sense.

"Demitri is enchanted by my blood, not my body nor my spirit. He has no interest in me other than to kill me and finish the job he so carelessly left alone this long." Mayline's loud voice was not betrayed by her shaking knees. Hellios chuckled as he shook his head, a small smile painting his pale lips.

He rested his chin on one palm, looking far younger

than Mayline knew him to be in that instance, and

lifted an eyebrow.

"What do you think of our dear Demitri,

Mayline Relix? Your creator and your Sire, but also

your enemy? Or perhaps your hatred is as misplaced

as you are right now? Would it be too painful to think

what would have happened had your precious little

Racelings not reached you in time? Or would it be as

exciting as I think it would? Because I have wondered

many times how you would have grown into such a

lovely Prime Vampire, Mayline...

"So often I have imagined you as one of us completely, fully by my side, wreaking havoc upon the world above. Have you not had the temptation to allow Demitri to sink his teeth into you once again, allow him to finish what he started? Have you never had these thoughts, truly, little Raceling? Have you never heard this Call of your Sire? I doubt you can find a way to say you never have." Hellios adjusted his crown thoughtfully, gazing intently into the burning blue eyes of the girl before him.

Mayline's fists clenched, her nails digging into her palms painfully. Her lips curled back over her teeth. She shut her eyes, trying to block out the words of the man in front of her, that arrogant, ignorant, hateful, powerful man in front of her. He knew all the right buttons to press without even knowing her.

"I-" She took a deep breath, trying to ignore the crack in her voice. Hellios smiled. "I have considered what it would be like to be a Prime. I have thought about it a lot actually." She looked up at him, her blue crystal orbs swirling into the defiant blood red shards of fire once more. "And I know it would have been Hell. I would rather die than let my humanity be any more tainted than it is now. This place is everything I despise. and with God as my witness, I swear I will never fight for Hell's armies!"

Her voice was a deep growl, her body shaking slightly with her rage.

Hellios laughed again, this time deeper and more mocking.

"Please! If you truly believe that your precious God exists, then why am I here? Who in their right mind would allow me to live if they are supposedly so…" he paused, his lip curling in disgust as he nearly spat the word. "…Loving…?"

Mayline shook her head, shoulders slumping slightly as she found comfort and peace in the thought of her Savior.

"I do not pretend to know what goes on in His mind, Hellios, but I do know that He has a plan, and no matter what happens to us down here, He is looking out for our best interests. There is nothing you can say to make me not believe that." She lifted her chin and narrowed her eyes at the King of Hell with cool disinterest. Hellios rolled his eyes.

"I should know better than to try to open the eyes of a superstitious, religious fiend. Blane! I have grown bored. You may have her for your amusement. Just do not kill her before Demitri has a taste. He might miss her," Hellios said, humor tinting his tones. Blane grinned, turning to look at the brunette girl hungrily.

"Yes, Master," he replied, amber eyes zeroing

in on Mayline's face as she looked over at him.

Hellios waved a hand lazily and sighed.

"Oh, do take her away now, Blane. The sight

of her offends me. Take her to the pits."

Mayline turned around quickly, but Blane was

already beside her. The tip of his steel-toed boot hit

the side of her head, and her vision went dark once

again.

Hands beat against the solid wooden door,

stirring Jordan from her lover's arms. Harvey groaned

and turned over, one wing coming to block out the

light and the sound. Jordan sighed and ruffled her

feathers as she stood. Her nightgown was pulled over

her form, covering her from the prying eyes of the

world. She rested a hand on the door frame, peering

between the boards to see who was disturbing her

rest.

She flung the door open as her wings spread,

her hair falling partially from the bun she had been

sleeping in. The noise had Harvey up and stepping

out of bed hurriedly. Jordan looked between Rachelle

and Rae with her silver eyes freezing over in dread.

"Where is Mayline?"

Chapter 11

The Ring

Mayline cracked her eyes open. Her body

ached all over, her hands clasped in front of her with

a pair of shackles. Her eyes fluttered closed again,

only to be opened a few seconds later as she felt

herself being dragged across the ground. Heavy hands

slid up her legs to her hips, clasping at her belt. Panic

set into her, clenching her heart in a suffocating grip.

She kicked out, hitting something hard and getting a

curse as a reward. Mayline attempted to crawl away

from her attacker, but he grabbed her again and

dragged her back toward him, her top riding up her stomach as the blood from the ground stained her pale skin.

"Not so fast, little scum-blood! I was going to keep you alive as my little pet, but since you have no manners, it seems like you need to be taught a lesson!" Blane's voice hissed into her ear. Mayline jerked, trying to break his hold but he was too strong. He dragged her up and yanked her around to attach her shackle to a chain hanging from the distant ceiling. He left her standing there for a moment to pull a lever off to the side. Slowly, the chain started retracting back into the ceiling.

Mayline jerked against the bindings, but she was soon dragged toward an open pit. She hovered at the edge of the pit for a moment before the chain pulled her over the edge. She swung violently as the chain pulled her arms above her head as it raised her slowly over the pit. Blane pulled the lever again, halting her ascent.

"Now then, you'll see just what comes of those who anger the Primes of Hell!"

Below her, fires erupted from the pit, licking up the air towards her legs. Mayline lifted her legs up to her chest to avoid being burned until the flames settled down enough for her to let her legs drop again.

Mayline winced. The blood dripping from her arm landed on her chin as she looked up at her bound hands. Her feet dangled over the pit, heat from the fire slowly cooking her skin. As she looked at her hands again, Blane laughed.

"Deny it to yourself all you like, scum-blood, but your Creator has abandoned you to the pits of Hell! None can save you now! You will burn just as we have!" the Prime shouted from his spot in the large chair placed on the rocks. Mayline growled.

"Shut up, Blane! All you are is the Devil's

bitch! The Creator never forgets his children! Our prayers are heard no matter where we are when we say them! This fire may eat my body, but my soul will never be taken, my heart will never be broken, and my faith will never be shaken!" she shouted back, anger and pain lifting her voice in volume.

Blane growled and raised his hand, a curse bubbling his skin like boiling water. The curse spilled from his palm, shooting toward Mayline.

"Your faith means nothing here! Your body will boil before it burns!" he cried over the sound of Mayline's sudden scream as her flesh started to bubble, the heat making her skin steam.

Mayline clenched her teeth then, refusing to give the Tracker the satisfaction of her screams. She screwed her eyes shut to keep out the image of her skin bubbling and popping, leaving open wounds to bleed across her body.

Blane laughed cruelly from his position on the dark chair, his feet resting on the lever that had raised Mayline by the chain. A wicked grin spread across his features, and he slowly moved his feet to the side, pushing the lever back the way it had come. Mayline jerked in the air, her screams turning to painful groans as more of her skin popped like blisters, as the chain slowly lowered her into the pit of fire. She struggled against the chain, trying to pull herself up toward the ceiling.

The shackles prevented her from moving her wrists efficiently. Frantically trying to raise her legs above the hungry fires licking at her toes while still suffering from the curse's painful malevolence, Mayline raised her voice in angry defiance, gripping the chain in both hands and pulling herself up. Gaining a few inches, she pulled again and let go, her momentum allowing her to grab a higher piece of chain.

Blane stared open-mouthed in amazement as this little chit of a girl managed to avoid being dipped in fire by climbing one of Hell's endless chains. Mayline swung her legs up, wrapping her ankles around the chain and gripping tightly. She let her hands fall from the chain, leaving her hanging by her feet over the fires for a moment before she hurled her body upward toward the chain by her ankles. She caught the metal in her hands, slipping slightly due to the blood pouring from her wounds, and heaved herself upward again.

"You will not escape!" Blane yelled angrily and stood, shoving the lever all the way down.

Mayline and the chain dropped like a lead weight straight into the fire.

Papers flew across the floor as they were hit away from the desk in a frantic gesture. Jordan, Harvey, Rae, Jennifer, and Rachelle stood around the table, each one thinking frantically.

Jordan, now clothed in her golden armor, turned to face Jennifer, her silver eyes boring into the younger woman earnestly. Jennifer shifted uncomfortably, the heaviness of the stare bringing unease into her core.

"You said two Hell Gates were opening around the same time? How soon until the next one opens? And where exactly is it?" Jordan asked, quelling any questions about actions to take before they were even asked. Jennifer stood straighter, staring straight ahead.

"Ma'am, the next Hell Gate is located in New Orleans, Louisiana, and should be open in three days," she said, her eyes never wavering but her voice cracking at the amount of time they would need to wait to attempt rescuing Mayline. Jordan dropped her shoulders in defeat.

"Three days…. Three days of her stuck in Hell, probably at Hellios's mercy… I don't… I can't…" Harvey walked up behind Jordan and wrapped her in his arms, his wings spreading around them both protectively.

"Do not worry, dear, we will get her, I promise. Mayline will not be there for that long. We will figure this out, I swear to you," he murmured reassuringly into her ear. Jordan clenched her eyes and nodded slowly, common sense warring with the trust she had in her mate. She sighed heavily and turned to look at Rachelle and Rae.

"Tell me, exactly, what Demitri said."

Mayline opened her eyes and looked around. Her hands were still tied, but they no longer hung above her. She coughed heavily, smoke stinging her throat. Blood pooled on her tongue. She wiped a palm over her lips and stared at the red liquid, slowly burning with the mix of her venom. She raised a lip in disgust and rubbed the soiled hand on her pant leg. She stood slowly, her arms limp at her sides, and turned in a circle to look around her.

She was in what seemed to be an endless void,

red tingeing her vision. A red gaseous horizon greeted her no matter where she looked. Hadn't she fallen into a fire? Why wasn't she burning alive? Or dead? Can you even die in Hell? Was it possible? Mayline bit her lip and took a hesitant step forward.

The landscape shifted suddenly from hazy red to pitch black, the space directly beneath her was pavement but outside a small radius around her was blackness. She stepped over the edge of the circle, but it moved with her, illuminating more of the ground at her feet. With another step, it happened again. She slowly continued to walk, the chain dragging behind her, never pulling against her wrists or hindering her movement. She looked around, her head turning a bit to glance over her shoulder.

Mayline paused, confused. Where she had come from, the empty space was filled. There were walls now, brick and plaster walls on either side of where she had started. She turned forward again, and she saw the walls in front of her as well. Confused, she reached out with her hands to touch the nearest wall, checking its existence.

The stone felt slimy and wet, cold to the touch and like it had rained recently. She sniffed, scrunching her nose. The dank smell that permeated from the walls was somewhat... familiar. She turned again to face where she had come. On the walls now were small lamps, one illuminated and the other dark and broken open. Mayline shuddered, not liking this particular feature of her current predicament, and turned to continue forward. She froze, her breathing choked off by a strangled sob of anguish and surprise. Before her, standing in the alleyway, she now recognized all too well, was her mother.

Mayline shut her eyes against the vision of her mother with blood coating the entirety of her front, and her throat ripped apart.

"Mayline... Little Mayline...." A sing-song voice whispered into the air. Mayline cringed, her teeth clenched, and her eyes shut.

"No! No, you aren't real! You are dead, you cannot be real!" she hissed, dropping to her knees and burying her head into her arms, the shackles preventing her from clutching at her ears to block out the sound of her mother's voice.

"You couldn't save us," a disembodied male voice said harshly. She flinched and looked up into the glassy eyes of her father. The open wound on his neck looked festered, but it was still noticeably a bite.

Mayline looked away but cried out as she saw the

legs of her older brother beside her, closer than her

father was. She looked up at him and screamed.

His eyes were white completely, having rolled

back into the sockets, and his lips were pale with his

skin paler. His lovely dark hair was matted with

blood, sticking to his forehead and cheeks.

Mayline clenched her eyes shut, refusing to

see any more, but the darkness that was welcomed by

her was broken. Her brother's face, eyes hollow and

mouth wide with blood painting his teeth and chin

red, flashed behind her eyelids, and the noises of the

world she was in were drowned out by his screams.

Mayline opened her eyes with a shriek and clawed away from her dead family. She turned her broken body away, and the alley was gone. Now she was in a forest, trees surrounding her in a cacophony of brown and green. The sunlight drifting between the branches of the trees was tinged red.

She recognized this forest. The Hide... She turned around quickly, looking for the doorway to safety. But as she turned, the trees caught fire, burning around her. She could see hundreds of people, faces she knew and recognized, screaming as they were torched alive in the bonfire.

"No! NO!" she screamed, trying to run forward. She tried to lift her feet to run to aid those she could, but her feet wouldn't move. She looked down, and horror flooded her. The ground was slowly swallowing her feet, creeping up her legs, pulling down. She tried to wrench her foot out of the quicksand-like earth but to no avail. She looked up frantically- just in time to see the burning body of Jordan collapse in front of her, screaming in agony. Mayline's eyes overflowed with tears at the horrifying sight of her beloved mentor burning to death just feet in front of her. Hopelessness invaded her, drenching her heart and covering her. She let the earth take her.

As the ground came up to block her nose and mouth, sand and dirt beginning to fill her eyes, she embedded the image of her burning haven in her mind, swearing to never allow it to happen. The earth closed entirely around her, not a hair left free. She could feel the soil moving around her, but her nose and mouth were blocked. Her lungs cried out for breath. Her vision went black.

Chapter 12

Demitri

Mayline's eyes fluttered open slowly. Around her, there was darkness with a small strip of light illuminating her surroundings. She lay on the plush blankets of a feather bed, sprawled uncaringly across the mattress. She took a deep breath, relieved at the feeling of her lungs expanding and turned her gaze to peak from between the curtains. The interior was dimly lit and dark in color, deep burgundy painting the walls. Black drapes hung from the bed frame, a canopy of jet blocking off her view of most of the room. A door on the far side was barely visible. She

slowly sat up, her muscles unusually loose and calm.

She remembered the earth swallowing her,

suffocating her. Was that all a dream? Was she still in

Hell?

She slowly reached for a curtain, pulling it

aside enough for her to plant her feet on the ground.

She stood slowly, cautious of making too much noise.

This room was unfamiliar, and therefore she

proceeded to softly rise and glance around.

There could be traps just waiting for her to

trigger them. Mayline lifted a foot slowly and took a

hesitant step. She whirled around at the sound of a door opening and leaped agilely up onto the top of the black canopy. She gripped the edges of the bed frame and spread her body so she would not be noticed dipping the curtains.

The door fully opened, sliding across the plush carpet quietly. Footsteps moved into the room, closing the door softly, as if not to wake her. She heard the sound of a man clearing his throat and gulped. Whoever was with her could be anyone in Hell. Perhaps Blane had taken her here to have his way with her like Hellios said... She heard the sound of cloth over skin. Curiosity overtook her. She slowly pulled herself to peak over the edge.

A man stood at a dresser with his back facing

Mayline. He was shirtless, and she could see the

length of his fine leather belt loose about his hips. His

back was muscular, pale skin stretching over the taut

frame. His hips were small, but shoulders strong and

broad. His black hair fell to caress the nape of his

neck, inky in its color. Mayline bit her lip, willing

him to turn around so that she could see his face. She

shifted to get a better view and- the bed frame

creaked.

Mayline hastily ducked behind her cover once

again as the man paused.

"Mayline?"

That voice…

She heard footsteps coming closer to the bed,

going to the break in the curtain where she had exited.

"Mayline...?"

That *voice*…

He drew back the curtains, and the empty bed

was revealed. A confused hum and the curtains fell.

Mayline held her breath. She blinked away a drop of

sweat and listened to him turn around and go back to

the dresser. She lifted her head, careful not to move her body again. As the man passed by the mirror, she caught a glimpse of his face.

Fear and dread filled her at the sight of her Sire. Demitri stood at the dresser, his bare back facing her once again. Mayline bit her lip, her heart starting to beat wildly in her chest. There was no way he could not hear it by now. She blinked heavily, clenching her eyes as tight as they would go to clear her slowly blurring vision. When she opened them, Demitri was gone. Confused, Mayline glanced around the room. He was nowhere to be seen. Had he merely been a dream? A vision of Hell's making? She hesitantly shifted her weight to the left, and

something cold and soft touched her side. Freezing in

fear, Mayline slowly looked over her shoulder.

Red eyes stared into her own blue orbs,

amused.

"Hello, Mayline," Demitri said from where he

hung above her, his hands an inch below hers on the

rail and his elbow bent at her side. She screamed as

he grinned.

He let go of the rail, falling into her and

sending them both crashing through the canopy. They

fell onto the bed, Mayline wrestling with Demitri as

he attempted to pin her hands to the bed. She grunted,
raising her knee up to knee his side, but he caught her
leg with one hand and forced it back to the mattress.
She struggled a bit longer, but with his weight pinning
her down, there was nothing she could do but collapse
back onto the bed, panting. He had her pinned under
him securely enough that he could move his left hand.
He rested it on her throat gently.

"Are you done now, my little Bloodborne?" he
asked, caressing the scar on the right side of her neck
that had been left by his fangs so long ago. Mayline
glared at him.

"What do you want with me? Why am I here? Last I remember I-"

"Died. Yes. You did. But then again, one can never truly die in Hell." He smirked, leaning back and releasing her, climbing off of her and sitting at the edge of the bed. He seemed unconcerned of her possible attack. But Mayline knew better. This could be the chance she was waiting for to learn how to escape Hell. She sat up and crawled to her knees, watching him.

"What do you mean, you cannot die here?" she asked. He smiled at her with a small, near indulgent smile. Mayline's eye twitched. She did not care for that kind of look.

"Here, death is eternal. If you arrived in Hell, properly, then you should already be dead. Fortunate for you, the pits make no distinction in arrival," Demitri said, leaning back against the headboard of the bed. Mayline raised an eyebrow at his relaxed position.

"Why is that fortunate? Surely, if I did not arrive here 'properly' then I would be spat out back into the world, right?" Mayline asked, confused. Demitri shook his head and closed his eyes.

"It wouldn't matter if you lived an evil life and died, lived a kind life and were cursed, or were shoved through a portal. Once you are in Hell, you are here to stay. There is no escape," he said, his voice bitter. Mayline suddenly realized that Demitri might not have wanted to be a Vampire anymore than she had. To be damned against your will… For all she knew, he could have been a righteous man in his human life. Pity welled up in her kind heart.

"Demitri… You've been on earth. That's where we met. How did you escape? Why did you return?" A harsh bark of laughter burst from forth from his lips, his eyes opening as he grinned at her, his white teeth gleaming.

"There is no escape from Hell. There are temporary passages granted by Hellios, the king under Satan himself, but never permanent reprieve. I am allowed out of the pits for a few days at a time, a week if I've been good. But I must always return. His pets-" A sneer broke his lips. "-will not allow overtime on the surface." Mayline tilted her head.

"If you have been good…?" she asked. He looked away from her for a long moment before rolling away and standing up. He walked away from the bed, his shoulders hunched. He shook his head and placed a hand on his hip as he ran his fingers through his hair.

"Mayline, I never wanted to be this. I hope you can understand this. Please, do not hold my actions against me. I battle with my anger and cruelty on a daily basis. I never wanted to be... Evil... But, I'm sure you can relate when I say, the pull of the Races is strong. And I was always a feeble man, Mayline, even as a human. My soul was forfeit before my change was even complete. I do not delight in the things I do," he explained, straining to get the words out. Demitri had never shown her such emotion before. She had only ever seen his arrogance.

Seeing him this way now almost made him…
human.

"Regarding you specifically," he continued, "I hold the most regret. I had never tried to change someone before. If I had been allowed the choice, I would have killed you before I damned your soul as mine has been. But in the end, I succeeded only in thrusting you face-first into a war not meant to be fought by one so young... I am not a kind man, and for that I am sorry, but I am no monster, truly. The things I do are so that I may be granted the boon that is temporary freedom," he said.

Throughout his speech, he did not turn to meet her gaze, nor had he moved from his position, his palm still to his forehead, eyes clenched. Mayline sat for a long moment, drinking in his words. She knew it could all very easily have been a ploy to gain her trust, but somehow in her heart, she knew that he spoke the truth. She stood slowly, walking up behind him.

"Demitri..."

His eyes opened, but he did not turn. Demitri's heart would have been pounding at the sound of her voice so close. The moment of truth had arrived...

"I-"

Voices from down the hall, getting closer, interrupted her. Demitri spun around and grabbed Mayline's throat. She gasped, her eyes wide and her hands clawing at his wrist. His red eyes darkened menacingly as the door to his chambers opened. He turned and threw Mayline into the mirror, the glass shattering at her back and slicing through her skin as she fell. She heaved her chest, lungs eager for the putrid air wafting through the now open door. She looked up and met Demitri's eyes with her hurt and confused pair. His face held no emotion, regret or smugness was absent. He was apathetic to the lovely maiden bleeding on his chamber floor.

"Lord Demitri. Master Hellios wishes to see your prize," one of the eager, young looking Primes said. Demitri nodded. He strode toward her, ignoring her attempts to back away and cutting her body against the glass even more. He grabbed a fistful of her hair, her hands clutching at his wrist as he yanked roughly and started dragging her by her hair out of the bedroom. She shouted in pain as he dragged her over the glass. Tears welled up in her eyes, but she refused to allow them to fall. She kicked out at the younger Primes as they passed, but only managed to hit her foot against the doorframe. She cursed and tried to twist out of his grasp as they reached the hallway.

The hallway across from Demitri's chamber was a balcony overlooking a bottomless pit, doors, and rooms inlaid into the walls with walkways around the edges. As he pulled her further out, she could see the lake of fire far below them and grey stone building pulling up from the fleshy earth. Demons milled about, ignoring the souls that could be seen in the fires as they writhed in agony and screamed for help. Above, the other rings of hell could be seen, getting larger as they rose up. Each ring had chains crisscrossing the opening as a sort of net, human souls hanging from them in various states of torture as though they were flies caught in a spider's webbing.

Every now and then, drops of blood could be seen

falling from the upper layers into the burning pit

below.

She was dragged screaming, her throat

becoming raw. She could feel the eyes of Demons,

Changelings, Primes of every Race upon her as

Demitri - damn him - dragged her toward a staircase.

He pulled her up by the hair and tossed her down the

stairs, glass shards getting shoved deeper into her

body. Demitri slowly walked down the steps toward

her, his eyes cold and vacant. Mayline looked up at

him, betrayal in her eyes. To think she had trusted

him of all people.

"Come now, Mayline, is that any way to look at your sire? He gave you this life!" a Prime to her left sneered. Mayline glared at him, tears welled but refusing to fall.

"He cursed me, you mean!" she hissed. Demitri glared at her.

"I gave you a gift."

"Then let me return the favor!" Mayline rose shakily to her feet and lunged at him. Demitri casually sidestepped her assault and swiped a hand at her back and pushing her face-first into the stairs. She hit her head on the carved rocks, and her vision went

dark.

Chapter 13

The Blame Game

Rae beat her bloodied hands against the stone

wall, froth dripping from her lips. Behind her,

Rachelle was frozen in place, her eyes unseeing.

Slowly, her heaving sobs filled the air alongside Rae's

roar of rage and helplessness. Letting out a final

scream, she could feel her vocal cords tense to the

point of pain. Her voice broke, and she collapsed onto

her knees in front of the portal that had swallowed her

friend. They had tried everything to open it once

again, but it had closed near instantly after Mayline

was thrown through. Demitri and the remaining

Primes had vanished out the high window, running

off to wherever they could return to Hell without the

portal. There was no trace left of them once Rae and

Rachelle had returned to attempt to open the Hell

Gate again.

They had been trying for hours. Days after

losing Mayline, they were still working. Not even

Rachelle's Demon form had aided them.

Rae spun around and howled again, her

yellow eyes bloodshot from the tears still streaming

down her face. Her teeth gleamed in the dull light cast

by the moon.

"It was a trap!" she growled, her voice harsh. "They didn't even need a portal! They even sent out Demitri to lure in Mayline! This entire thing was a trap, and we fell right into it!" Rachelle groaned and leaned against the wall, her body shaking in misery as she slid down the stone to sit in a tiny ball. Her bones slowly slipped back into her human form, her skin returning to its normal lightly tanned tone, but her face still looked ashen as she looked up at Rae once more. Tears dripped from her eyes, leaving wet trails down her cheeks. She made no move to clear them and merely sat there, her eyes glazing over.

Rae punched the wall again, the room shaking

with the force of the wolf's anger.

Demitri had done the near impossible.

He had incited her rage.

She lay flat on the stairs as those around them

laughed, called her weak; spat into her hair as she lay

defenseless and injured. Demitri did not laugh, he did

not speak, but she could feel his eyes burning her,

drinking in the sight of her broken body.

Mayline clenched a single fist. She had to do

something. In open combat, she would be overrun in seconds. But she was a Vampire. Vampires did not need open ground to call a battle victorious.

She held her breath and rolled over, vaulting into the stone rafters.

Those below howled in anger, some jumping up to follow her, but she had learned well. She melted into the shadows so deep even their Prime eyes could not see clearly. She slithered along the stones, her fingers gripping the beams tightly. She lifted her body into a handstand, her feet touching another rafter above her. She wrapped her ankles around it and pulled herself up, trying not to breathe.

On the beam she had been on seconds before, a wolf jumped up and clawed at it, trying to stay on it while it tracked her scent. Mayline grinned. She gripped the beam she was on in her hands, swinging her legs down to kick the mutt in the face and knocking it into the wall across the room. It slid down, unconscious. Her momentum carried her back up to rest her feet on the beam, and she jumped away to another quickly as the Primes rushed to the area.

Demitri watched in fascination as one by one each of the Primes fell to the hands of the injured girl in the rafters. How they did not see her in the

shadows was beyond him. Their eyes were better than

hers... Weren't they?

Mayline gritted her teeth as she hung upside

down from a beam, her nails digging into the hard

stone like it was butter. Below her, two Demons were

looking down from the beam they were on. She

couldn't touch them directly, their spines were too

long. But maybe...

She dropped down to the beam behind the

two, her feet silent in the stillness. Calls of other

Primes were the only sounds as they searched for her.

Mayline's eyes locked on the weak spot Rachelle had told her about. She reached up and tore two chunks of the stone beam out, the crack drawing the attention of the searchers.

As they started turning around, Mayline threw both rocks as hard as she could, aiming for the small area where the spinal bones stopped, and the tailbone had not started yet. Her aim was true, and both Demons howled in pain as they dropped from the beam, bones breaking on impact with the floor.

Mayline hurdled down onto the floor and sprinted across the hallway to the stairs where

Demitri was. He was so stunned by her lack of care

for those who spotted her, he did not move. She had

almost reached him when she leaped straight over

him, hitting the landing below him and rolling to the

side to continue down the stairs.

As she reached the floor below, she jumped

into the rafters again. She would do this for as long as

she could. Her partially human eyes adjusted to the

lack of light, bolstered by the venom in her blood.

The Primes could not see her because it took longer

for their eyes to adjust, but when they did, they would

be able to see ten times better than she could. She had

to act fast, switch from dark to light quickly enough

that they were kept off balance, in the limbo of vision.

She twisted her body and pushed herself up to the highest rafter possible. There was only one. She could not remain there long. Primes poured down the stairs, over the edge of the walkway, up from lower floors. There were too many even for her. A Banshee breathed fire up toward the ceiling, illuminating the rafters below Mayline. She cursed her poor luck and jumped to a lower beam, trying to find a way out of the corner she had found herself in.

There were hundreds of them. The only way out would be straight through their ranks. They blocked the stairs, the balcony, everything. And even if she could get through them and to the balcony, she would be hurling herself into a pit of fire and brimstone. The only option she had was to force her way through the swarms and hope for the best. If she didn't make it... There was no other choice. She had to at least try. Her courage would fail her if she tried to think about it more.

Mayline leaped to another beam. Her foot slipped on something wet on the stone, forcing her to wrap her arms around the stone to keep herself from falling.

She carefully maneuvered herself to kneel on the beam, panting softly. Then she froze. Something hot and wet dripped onto her neck from above. It ran over her throat and dropped onto her hand. It was clear. She looked up… into the yellow eyes of a Werewolf.

Jennifer was no fool, but she held in her heart a fool's hope. There had to be a way to get Mayline out of Hell. Jordan sat in front of Jennifer, her head in her hands, feathers ungroomed… Her wings hung limply at her sides, refusing to stand proudly as they usually did. Jennifer stared at the matron in both

remorse and slowly fading shock. Since Mayline had

been lost, Jordan blamed herself.

"Jordan…" she mumbled. The Angel shook

her head slowly and lifted her head to meet Jennifer's

eyes with her own bloodshot gaze.

"I sent her to that castle, Jen. I sent her to her

death," Jordan murmured. Jennifer shook her head

quickly, coming to Jordan's side to rest her hands on

her mentor's shoulders.

"Jordan, you did what you thought was best.

She isn't dead-"

"She's in Hell, Jennifer! There's no coming back from that!"

The sound of skin on skin flashed suddenly in the room, and Jennifer reeled back, her palm stinging. Jordan stared at the floor, her head still turned from the force of the slap. Her eyes were wide and unseeing.

"Don't you *dare* say that! She isn't dead, she isn't gone! We can still get her out!"

"How?! How can we break into Hell itself and get someone out, physically? Only Hellios himself and the Beast can allow anyone to leave!" Jennifer blinked.

"Say that again." Jordan looked up at Jennifer

confused. Then her eyes lit up.

"The Beast."

<u>Chapter 14</u>

Red

Her eyes opened, slowly; awakening to the

world of color turned to pitch. She moaned and

slowly rolled onto her side. The ground beneath her

was cold and hard, covered in a thin layer of dust.

Her tongue wet her lips, tasting the dust on the pink

flesh. She blinked, and a cloud of dust floated from

her skin to rest on the floor below her. She flicked her

gaze around the room, clearing, place that she was in.

It was dark, lit only by twin torches on either side of

her. She sat up, her legs swinging over the edge of

the… altar? Why was she sleeping on an altar? The torches flared as her feet touched the ground.

Suddenly, the room around her was illuminated by thousands of small fires, torches hung from the ceiling of the circular room she stood in the center of. She turned on her toes, trying to keep up with the lighting torches. The room was filled with pews; aisles mimicking a church. Her body twisted around to try and see everything.

Behind her, between two torches, a door slid open. Through it, stepped a man in priest's clothing, holding a lantern aloft with a small flame *illuminating his face. He looked up at her, surprised.*

"You're awake." It wasn't a question. There was no room for an explanation as he quickly shuffled up to the altar. "When did you wake up?" he asked. She shook her head, her voice too ancient to be used. The priest, for there was no doubt he was of the cloth, beckoned her forward, bowing slightly to her as she stepped toward him.

"My lady, you are the one we have waited for. Please, come with me, my queen." He turned and began walking toward the door he had entered through. As she followed him, her vision grew dark.

With every step, the world around her grew blurred.

With a heaved sigh, the world gave way, and she opened her eyes to stare into the face of her most hated enemy. The sun.

Wait. The sun? How was she outside? Why was she...? Oh. There was a window.

Rae groaned and slowly turned over in her bed, her will to move slowly draining from her body and her motivation to do her chores quickly fading as well. Cracking her eyes open, she glanced around her room, the window showing the sun instead of the full moon from the night before. She turned over, her back cracking with the movement, and let out a groan.

Her eyes were tired from the night before.

Rae rolled out of bed, trying not to make too

much noise. Other Raceling Werewolves were still

sleeping in their own pens. Rae reached out of the

bars of her pen and pulled the rope, calling for help.

Her handler walked into the room with the key to her

pen. Rae watched the key turn, ready to bolt but

fighting the instinct. Her body tensed as the door

opened. The entire world turned yellow and her

handler dived out of the way as Rae rushed out of the

cage, her hands turning into claws that she slashed at

the air in freedom. The other Werewolves opened

their eyes, howling as she lifted her voice in victory.

Jennifer rested her head on the glass of the window beside her, the hum of the engine making her forehead vibrate slightly. Beside her, Jordan drove the van full of Racelings trying to save the newest victim. A young Hispanic girl, whose color was slowly fading as her spirit was drained from her by the Banshee inside her. Jennifer looked back, watching the life force slowly fading as the squadron realized they had arrived too late.

"If you cannot save her," Jordan said, her jaw

tight and her eyes tired. "Then kill her."

Jennifer whirled to face Jordan, but her mouth refused to form the words in her heart. *Give her a chance.* Jordan did not move. *Please... Jordan. Not all of them have to be evil...* But it was no use. A shrill cry of anguish filled the van as the girl and the Banshee inside of her were killed with a holy knife to the chest. Jennifer felt the Banshee die, the force of the released spirit shaking her body.

Not every Prime is evil.

Mayline spat out blood, wiping a palm across

her lips to rid herself of the remnants. She sent a glare

to the wall where the window was. She could feel the

stares from the other side of the window, watching

her. They were testing her. She did not know why or

for what she was being tested, but they were. Mayline

twisted, looking at her opponent. The Changeling

woman stood unharmed, but emotionless. Her skin

was slowly becoming scales. Mayline tried to guess

what creature she could be shifting into but came up

with a blank as the scales began turning yellow.

Whatever this was for, she could not fail this

test. She had no confirmation but the feeling in her

gut that if she failed… she would die. She lunged

again, and hit the Changeling head on. Mayline

twisted, trying to dodge the gaping jaws of the now

fully transformed boa constrictor. She flipped to the

side and growled, the sound vibrating deep in her

chest. Her eyes, normally blue and clear, slowly

turned a bright ruby red. Her pupils dilated, the

crimson irises taking over the whites of her eyes. Her

lips pulled back over her glistening teeth as her growl

got louder. She opened her mouth wide and hissed at

the snake as it slowly slithered toward her.

Mayline was no longer a Raceling. Her Race

had taken over her mind. She saw red.

She lunged.

Her fist collided with the Changeling's face, sending the creature flying back into the wall. Before she had a chance to recover, Mayline sprinted toward her at top speed, becoming a blur as she did. Claw like hands gripped the Changeling's throat, digging in so deep that blood erupted around her fingertips.

Mayline snarled, her teeth elongating into fangs and gleaming with the silvery venom of her Race. She snapped at the Changeling before turning and flinging her across the room. The wall cracked under the hit. The Changeling tried to pick herself up, but Mayline was already at her side again, grabbing

her coils, picking her up, and slamming her into the

wall again, forcing the snake back into a woman. The

Changeling clutched her head and shook, trying to

clear her eyes.

Mayline smiled, the corners of her mouth

beginning to tear as her jaw opened wide, venom

dripping in thick strands from her teeth. The

Changeling screamed and tried to scratch at Mayline's

face. The Vampire, for Mayline had no trace of

humanity left anymore, hissed slowly, the sound

matching itself to the whimper of the Changeling. The

screech that filled the room as Mayline's teeth tore

into the Changeling's throat was bloodchilling, even

for the onlookers.

The blood poured into Mayline's mouth,

tasting of the different species the Changeling had

taken the forms of. She swallowed the sweet nectar as

she let the corpse fall from her hands. Her eyes slowly

returned to normal as she panted, her shoulders

heaving and the blood dripping from her heavily. She

turned to the window and her still feral eyes locked

on the figure through the glass.

Mayline slowly came back to her senses,

blinking every time her fists collided with the

reinforced glass, trying to break through. Her

breathing was ragged and sharp pain in her side let

her know that her lungs were protesting the

hyperventilation. Her knuckles hit glass again, blood

dripping from her fingers. Blood that was not hers.

Her vision went red once again before clearing with

her other hand being pulled away from the glass.

When had she punched with that one? She took a step

back, clutching at her head. It felt like her blood was

on fire, like there was something in her veins trying to

take control, trying to take the last shreds of her

humanity.

She screamed in pain, dropping to her knees

and clutching at her hair, eyes clenched shut and head shaking rapidly. The window darkened and the wall opened to let Demitri and Hellios into the room. They watched Mayline claw at her skin, blood dripping from the cuts and bubbling on the floor. Demitri eyed the droplets as the venom in her blood turned the red liquid into a puddle of ooze.

"It appears that the incompetent Racelings were correct for once. Her Race-level is extremely high, Demitri. Higher, it would seem, than even the first Raceling," Hellios observed, leaning down to press a finger to the black blood on the floor. The liquid began to steam on contact with his cool flesh.

Chapter 15

Reunion and War

She needed to stop passing out. It probably

was really bad for her, though she supposed it was the

only sleep she was allowed in Hell. She blinked at the

shackles holding her suspended from the stone floor

of the throne room of Hellios. Mayline tried to look

around, but her head was held in place by a steel

collar wrapped around her throat. There was a muzzle

over her mouth that prevented her from opening her

mouth wide enough to bite anything. They had really

pulled out all the stops to contain her this time. Her

crystal blue eyes scanned the room, darkening as they landed on the brazier filled with green fire and two long metal poles. Mayline rolled her eyes. This again.

"Oh, do not worry, Miss Relix. Those aren't for you." She flicked her eyes to look at the figure of Hellios standing beside her. His smile was cold and unfriendly, and behind him, his golden wings were unfurled entirely. The feathers moved slightly in the wind from a door opening somewhere behind her. Footsteps had Hellios turning toward the newcomer.

"Is he ready?" he asked. The newcomer silently replied, and Hellios smiled widely at Mayline.

Something in that smile made her blood freeze in her veins and heavy dread settled in her breast. "Bring him in."

Four sets of steps entered the room then, one more being dragged along with them. Three people entered her vision, two of them were dragging the third by the arms. There was a sack over the head of the prisoner. He was forced to his knees in front of Mayline, facing her. Then the sack was ripped off his head.

Mayline let out a scream that made her throat bleed. Tears welled up in her wide, crazed eyes and she jerked against her restraints. Her screaming was

nearly feral at the sight in front of her. It was

Donovan. Her brother.

"Donny!" Her voice was hoarse from

screaming. Her brother was kneeling in front of her

between two Prime bastards who each now held a red

hot pole close to his body. She knew he recognized

her, even through the dirt and the blood and the chains

covering her.

"May!" His voice echoed in her mind. Images,

real and fiction, flitted through her mind - her brother

lying dead at her feet, eyes glazed; the zombie-like

form of him crawling toward her. The images flashed

faster. Mayline screamed, her blood boiling under her

skin.

The chains holding her snapped, her fingers

landing in one of the Primes' throat before she could

even register that she was free. She turned her hands

outward and ripped them out of his neck, sending his

head flying back and his body slumping at her feet.

The head rolled. The next instant, her fingers

squelched through the eyes of the second Prime.

His screaming didn't make her other hand

hesitate as she forced her clawed fingers through the

side of his skull. She felt the bone break under the

motion, and her fingers squelched into his brain. Grey

matter dripped from her fingers in large chunks as she

ripped out both hands, the force of the movement

sending the body into her chest. The blood smeared

onto her clothes as she pushed it off of her.

Mayline turned around slowly, teeth bared and

eyes blood red, looking at each of the seven Primes in

the room. Hellios was smiling too much for someone

who just lost two soldiers in less than five minutes.

Mayline paid little attention to the lesser beings,

focusing solely on the winged maniac that had her

brother's soul. She took a step toward him, growling

deep in her chest, the sound loud enough to reach the ears of the Primes standing across the room by the door. Hellios chuckled and raised his hand towards her.

"My dear little Raceling, you have finally unlocked your full potential. I knew you were special," he said. Mayline blinked, eyes slowly returning to their normal crystal blue, though the usually golden ring around her pupil remained red. She took a step back, unsure now, though she stayed between her brother and Hellios.

"What do you mean?" she asked, despite her

hesitation. Maybe if she got him talking, she could figure out a way to escape. Hellios chuckled.

"Child, you are more powerful than you realize - than any of the Racelings realize. Usually, it takes the Sire completing the transformation for a Raceling to draw on the full potential of their Race. But you? You do not need that. With your Race-level, all you need is a little push in the right direction, and eventually, your blood will be consumed by the venom completely, and you will be one of us."

Mayline's head pounded, her vision went blurry, she could hear the beating of her heart in her ears, and it felt like the walls of the palace were

crashing in on her.

"No," she murmured, shaking her head in

denial. Hellios laughed heartily, his wings ruffling as

he threw back his head.

"Child, you can deny it all you wish, but you

cannot stop your destiny!" Mayline screamed and

charged him.

Hellios spread his wings and dodged her hand

as she clawed toward his face. He lept over her and

swiped a wing into her back, sending her flying into

the wall ahead of her. She cracked the stone and slid

down, blood pooling from her lips. She rolled into a

crouch and growled, swiping a hand across her mouth

to rid herself of the sizzling blood. Hellios heaved his

shoulders, and the momentum sent him toward her,

his hand reaching forward to grasp at her. Mayline

rolled to the side and hit the wall, her feet finding a

perch on the corner of the wall. Hellios turned, his

wings flapping so hard the wind pushed the other

occupants of the room away. Mayline growled as she

watched the Fallen Angel come toward her. She

raised her arm to block, but she was too slow.

Hellios slammed into her, his forearm locking

her arm to her chest. Her back hit the wall with a loud

crack as the stone crumbled under the force. She felt a few ribs crack. Blood dripped from her lips, and she coughed, eyes wide and staring into the golden gaze of the king. His face was twisted into a sick grin, teeth bared as though to bite her.

Mayline lifted her other hand and grabbed his shoulder, pulling him closer to her.

"Face it, girl. You are no different than any Prime here. You are no different than I!" he growled out through his clenched teeth.

"The difference-" she coughed, "between you and me… Is that I know how to dance," she hissed, blood splattering across his face.

Mayline twisted her hips and lifted her legs, locking her ankles around Hellios's back. She dragged him closer to her with a sudden, strong jerk and ducked her head as his forehead jolted toward her. His skull cracked against the wall, and the shock caused the rest of the ruined wall to crumble underneath them both. Mayline brought her legs up toward her chest, sending her legs out with force and Hellios went spinning toward the ground as she rolled away. His head hit the stone floor with a loud thunk, and he rolled forward until he rested on his back. Mayline panted painfully, gripping her torso as she lay on her back on the shattered stones. Hellios was

motionless. Mayline silently thanked Jordan for

insisting that dancing lessons would be good for her

flexibility.

She heard the sound of multiple people

running toward her and groaned. She kicked a leg up

and rolled backward onto her knees, her head coming

up to face the three Primes rushing toward her. With a

glance behind her to make sure Hellios was still out,

she hopped onto her feet again, ignoring the pain that

came with breathing and braced herself for impact. As

the first Prime - a massive man with bulging muscles

in his neck and forearms the size of cannonballs - was

almost upon her, she jumped up, feet landing

perfectly on his bulging shoulders and flipped over

the other two. She hit the ground running.

Three shouts of outrage followed as she

skidded to a halt beside her brother.

"Don't worry, I'll get you out of here. Just

hold still and don't breathe too heavily." She lifted

one of the chains holding him and locked her fingers

into the metal. With the sounds of the Primes'

approach in her ears, she twisted the heavy link until

it snapped. She lifted the heavy chain up and turned

around as it dropped from one of her brother's arms,

swinging the chain out to catch another, smaller and apparently faster Prime in the jaw, sending him to the ground with a loud crack.

She hefted the chain again and ran to meet the other two. She hopped to the side as the big guy's hand shot out toward her and wrapped the chain around his forearm. She spun away and slid between the other Prime's legs with the chain, pulling the bigger one's arm around to smack into the other's chest.

They went down in a tumble, and Mayline rolled up, using the end of the chain to crack them both on the temple before dropping it. The small

Prime was getting up, holding his shattered jaw

gingerly. Mayline rushed him, not waiting to see if he

would give up. She leaped at him, nails clawing into

his flesh and ripping open his skin from his neck to

his chest. She hit the ground and rolled, wiping his

blackened blood on her pants as he fell face forward

onto the stone.

Standing straight, she panted, watching the

Primes for any sign of movement. Nodding at the

unconscious trio, she turned to look over at where

Hellios - pain shot through her as the fist collided

with her jaw. She went flying two hundred yards back

into the opposite wall. The stone crumbled and she skidded into another room.

Mayline struggled to stay breathing, her vision becoming blurry. Colors danced over her eyes as her head lolled to the side. A dark shadow covered her. Her eyes refused to focus on the figure above for longer than a second. Demitri was beside himself. Literally. She was seeing four of him. The images separated and came back together as he said something she could not hear over the ringing in her ears. She tried to make out the words his lips were forming, but she could not make the images stop swirling enough to focus. Her head was swimming, and her brain was throbbing. The grey matter seemed

to melt out of her ears. Her mouth was filled with

cotton.

"You are a tough one, for sure. Pity. You could

have been great."

Mayline's vision went dark, and she hit the

stone floor.

Get up!

Wake up!

Her eyes shot open, and she saw her own hands on the floor in her own blood. Mayline looked up quickly, fast enough to see the kick to her head before it hit. Not, however, quick enough to dodge it. His foot smacked into her face and cracked her teeth together. She went flying into the wall. Again. She was starting to get tired of being beaten up.

"Alright," she said, "This is getting really old." She wiped the blood from her lips and stood straight. Her fists were clenched and shaking with rage. Her vision started to bleed into burgundy as the pain in her head began to drain away. Her fangs lengthened, and her jaw dropped, nearly unhinged.

With a roar, she leaped forward and reached her hands

out to claw at Demitri. He backhanded her hard

enough to send her head twisting around, but her nails

dug into his collarbone. She managed to rip a chunk

of his flesh off as she went flying. He howled in pain,

clutching his hand to his shoulder. He cursed at her

and lunged.

He was interrupted in his charge by one of the

chains being flung at him. They knocked him out of

the air, and he hit the ground. Mayline was grabbed

from behind, and she whirled around, ready to fight.

Her brother looked back at her, slightly translucent,

tugging at her arm.

"Let's go!" he yelled and started dragging her out of the room. She followed without a second thought. This was her big brother. He'd always protected her, and she had no reason to believe that now was any different. She followed him through the main doors and past the stairs.

"Where are we going?" she called up to him. He didn't stop or answer. Instead, he dragged her through two large gates. Mayline looked up as the screams reached her.

He had brought her to the racks.

Chapter 16

Desperate Measures

Mayline looked over at her brother, his face as grim as she would expect. He had brought her to the lower racks of the ninth ring. Physical torture was used in every ring, but this was different. This was body horror. Utter mutilation. When the bodies were too broken to continue, they were thrown into piles to heal until they could be tortured again. However, this small respite was equal torture as every muscle knit back together. The screams didn't end until the vocal cords were torn out.

Donovan glanced at her. Her face was pale as she looked at him. Something twisted in his gut and he reached for her. His nearly insubstantial body touched her shoulder, and she felt utterly cold where they touched.

"We have to be quiet. We can not be caught here, or this is where we will stay. The worst of the worst are being tortured here. We need to get up to the next ring, but we can't go through the city," he said. Mayline's brow furrowed.

"City? What city?" He pointed behind her, to the left of the door they had entered through. She looked, and her head slowly went upward, following

the towering buildings built into the wall of the ring.

The red, pulsating rock of the wall connected

seamlessly into the stone of the tall buildings.

Through the streets between them, Demons of every

kind walked. Each looked different, never two of the

same color or shape. Where one had spikes growing

from his spine, another had horns twisting out of the

exposed bone of her skull.

It was an entire sprawling city of Demons - a

bustling society built beside pits of torture.

Mayline looked back at her brother, shaking

slightly.

"What do we do, Donny?" she asked, voice small and timid. He straightened.

"We have to climb. Each ring is connected by the opening in the middle-" He pointed to the gaping hole in the ceiling where the top of a giant fire reached upward into the ring above them. "It'll be hard, nearly impossible, but we have to get you out of here. You don't belong here, May, so I'm gonna get you out." Mayline shook her head and grabbed her brother's shoulders.

"You don't belong here either, Donny, you

have to come with me!" she cried, desperation edging into her voice. Donovan shook his head and put his hands over hers on his shoulders.

"Sis, we don't have time to talk about why I'm here. We can do that when you are safely at a Hell Gate. Now come on, we have to go. They'll be looking for us. When they realize we aren't in the castle anymore, they will start looking for us in the city. We need to be as far from there as possible. Now, let's go."

Donovan pulled Mayline away from the door and away from the city, toward the racks of torture and the wall beyond. Behind them, inches from where they had been standing, two eyes opened in a section of the wall. They blinked and then moved off the wall, shaping into a Banshee with a wicked grin on her face. She tittered behind her delicate hand and moved down the stairs gracefully to tell her King where his prize was heading.

Jennifer shivered in the cold wind, her hair whipping around her like a hurricane. In front of her, Rachelle and Rae were kneeling in the dirt, pouring some kind of heavy white powder into a circle.

Rachelle directed her friend on how to draw the circle correctly, gesturing to the points where the star was to connect. Jennifer's cold hands fumbled with the black wax candles, trying to keep them all upright as she placed them on the uneven ground. Behind her, Alex and another Angel, Veronica, were surrounding the area with devil traps. What they were doing was incredibly dangerous and highly unlikely to work, but Jennifer was sure it was their only chance at saving Mayline.

"No, Jen, that's where the offering goes, not the last candle. You hold the last candle," Rachelle said, picking up the largest of the candles from the center of the pentagram. Carefully, she stepped out of the summoning circle and fished in her pockets for the lighter to light the candles.

"How do you know all this stuff?" Veronica asked.

"She probably does this shit all the time. Demon stuff and all," Alex scoffed and glared at Rachelle. Rachelle sent him a glare and huffed.

"It's Demonology 101, Vee. It comes ingrained once you're turned. One day it just pops into your head. Like how you guys know automatically how to use your staves and your Grace

Glow in battle. We just… know," Rachelle explained,

shrugging. "It comes in handy in times like this. I do

not necessarily approve of what we are doing, but if it

gets my friend back, I'll do anything." She tossed her

lighter to Rae and nodded. "Light 'em up, Wolfie."

Rae sent her a halfhearted glare but did as she

was told. Rachelle knelt in front of the now lit candles

and circle and picked up the silver bowl beside her.

She placed it carefully in the center of the ring and

cringed slightly away from it. Inside the dish was a

bloody heart torn from an ordinary wolf that Rae had

hunted and carved.

They had hung it up by the back legs and drained its blood into a sack, which she now used to fill a silver goblet. She set the goblet beside the heart and then reached for the silver plate with two halves of a pomegranate placed carefully upon it. Both halves were insides-down on the silver, the juice pooling under them. She set the plate on the other side of the bowl from the goblet and scooted away, still on her knees. A full meal for The Beast himself. She nodded briefly, surveying her work.

Finally, she picked up the large candle and lit it with one of the other candles.

"Everyone stand in a devil trap. I'm the only one he technically cannot possess, so you guys need to stay out of the way." As each of her companions stood in a devil trap, Rachelle glanced around the dark clearing. The trees moved with the rough winds, leaves rustling. There was no grass in the clearing. They had traveled a long way to find the place called The Devil's Stomping Ground, hoping it would be the most accessible place to summon him. Rachelle shivered. The place reeked of evil.

"What, exactly, do we want to ask of him?" she asked.

Jennifer was the first one to answer.

"We want Mayline back!"

Rachelle rolled her eyes.

"We need a direct request or deal to make with him, we can't just demand he gives her to us. What exactly do we want from him?"

Jennifer looked at the others as they looked to her expectantly. Obviously, it was her plan, it was her job to figure out what to say to the most evil thing alive or dead. Great.

"We would like to respectfully ask for him to

aid us in retrieving our friend from his realm,"

Rachelle said, encouragingly, nodding to Jennifer. Jen

nodded back, stuttering out her next words.

"We would like permission to walk through

his domain unharmed and unimpaired to retrieve her

if he is unable or unwilling to bring her to us

directly…" she said, searching for Rachelle's

approval of her idea. Rachelle thoughtfully chewed

her lip before nodding slowly.

"That could work… he may try to trick us

with that one though. Our best bet is probably just

asking for him to let her go. Or at least, if she's trying

to escape herself, call off his little minions. Hellios

may try to work around that though. Honestly, I'm

not totally sure what to say here that won't end up

biting our butts," she admitted, sighing. She drew

herself up, remaining on her knees but with a straight

back, and settled her face into a glare out into the

trees in front of her. She felt like she was being

watched. Like they all were.

    The trees moved with the wind, but nothing

moved between them. She tried to press the feeling

down, swallowing around the lump growing in her

throat.

"Alright. Let's summon The Beast."

Mayline's forehead was covered in droplets of sweat and blood as she and Donovan crept through the racks, hiding under the bodies being tortured. A man's intestines spilled out to her left, only to be stabbed and lifted up again by a Demon's pitchfork. She swallowed and tried not to look up. The naked bodies writhing above her were almost as bad as the screams. Donovan had her hand tightly in his as he led her through the mass of agony. Suddenly, through the other screams came a shrill cry of pain and fear. It was too young to be an adult. Mayline froze as the

unmistakable sound of a child cut through the air. Her

eyes traveled up of their own will and locked on the

writhing body of a little girl with a wooden pike

through her stomach.

Bile rose into her throat, and Mayline gagged.

Donovan spun around at the noise and followed her

eyes. Cursing softly, he tore off his vest and covered

his sister's eyes with it.

"Just keep moving," he murmured, pulling her

along again. "We can't save them."

She forced herself to keep crawling beside her

brother. She closed her eyes and latched a hand onto his ankle, allowing him to guide her with his own movements.

Behind her, the little girl screamed.

Chapter 17

The Beast

Rachelle's eyes were glowing a bright white as she spoke the incantation of summoning. The circle around her started glowing white to match her eyes. Magic flowed around her in wisps of energy, rippling like water over her skin. She felt powerful. She felt ethereal. She felt whole.

Suddenly, the white light shot up from the ground, forming a tube in the summoning runes. Rachelle finished the incantation, and a black hoof erupted from the light, followed by another. Horns poked through, and a massive body filled the circle.

The light dissipated and Rachelle heard her

companions let out different reactive noises. Gasps,

shouts, and a shrill scream.

Rachelle looked up at The Beast before her. Its

body was bloated and muscular, red skinned until the

neck and the waist. Its feet were backward hooves,

cloven and blackened with soot. Its head was that of a

lion with ram horns jutting from the top of the skull.

Its mouth hung open with slavering jowls and tusks

rising from the bottom set of teeth. Its eyes were

yellow with slitted pupils and drool dripped from its

mouth and to the ground. The soil where it hit burned.

Rachelle looked up at the monster in front of her, her heart beating in her throat. She swallowed and bowed her head.

"Lo-lord Beast… We c-come before you tonight to make a request." Rachelle's voice was shaking. She was terrified.

What request would you make of me, child?

The mouth of the great Beast did not move. The voice echoed through the trees and the gathered party's minds without any indication that the beast had spoken. Rachelle shivered.

"Our friend was captured and taken to Hell,

your realm. She was still alive and had yet to face

Judgement. We would ask for your help to return her

to us, or to allow us safe passage through your realm

to retrieve her."

You think I would relinquish a soul from

my lands? Taken by one of my Second's few

captains?

"We-well… Yes?" Rachelle looked back at

Jennifer then resolutely looked back at The Beast, no

longer bowing. "Yes."

The creature chuckled.

You are a fool to believe I would allow such

a thing.

"We do not require your permission," Alex said from his protective circle. The Beast swung its head to look at him, yellow eyes glowing.

And what authority would a blasphemous Angel have over me?

"Blasphemous?" Veronica looked up at Alex in disbelief. He glowered at The Beast without replying.

"Alex?"

"You are beholden to Heaven, are you not?"

Alex asked, raising his chin. Rachelle looked back at

the beast as a heady chuckle echoed through the air.

I am beholden to no one, boy. You should

watch your own tongue before dreaming of

someone else's.

Alex sputtered, and Rachelle whirled around

to look at him incredulously. Alex looked between

The Beast and Rachelle and glared at the Demoness.

"What are you looking at, bone-bitch?"

"Is now really the time for insults, guys?"

Jennifer shouted, throwing up her hands. Rachelle

rolled her eyes and looked back at The Beast.

"Please, we just want our friend back. She didn't even die, she was stolen from us by Demitri and -"

Demitri? Would your friend's name happen to be Relix?

"Uhm, yes?" Rachelle answered with a question, confused as to why Demitri's name had been the thing he latched onto.

You may have her.

Rachelle blinked. "Sorry, what?"

You may have your friend back. I shall send

her along shortly.

"Uhm… Why was that so easy?" Rae asked.

The Beast turned to her.

Your little friend has been wreaking havoc

on my armies in my own realm. I do not have time

for that shit. You can keep her.

Rachelle blinked, and her mouth dropped

open. The Beast let out a roar and fire erupted from

the ground to swallow it, taking it back to the pits.

Rachelle turned to look at her companions,

mouth still open in shock. Jennifer shook her head in

disbelief. Veronica and Alex looked at each other.

Rae let out a hysterical laugh and toppled over, her sides hurting with each breath. Every set of eyes turned to her as she dropped to her side on the ground and kicked her legs as she laughed. And laughed. And laughed.

"What," Alex began, "Is so fucking funny, mutt?"

Rae's laughter did not pause, but she managed to wheeze out words between gasps for breath.

"Not even the *Devil* wants to deal with Mayline on a mission!"

Jennifer covered her mouth with a hand to

hide a snort. Veronica giggled. Rachelle chuckled.

Alex burst out laughing.

Chapter 18

Redeemer

Mayline followed behind Donovan, finally free of crawling under the racks, as he climbed up a ridge of fleshy rocks. She grunted, wiping a hand on her shirt to remove the strange ooze that came from the rocks.

Donovan looked back and offered a hand. She took it. He raised her up, and they crawled over the edge of the ridge. Mayline rolled onto her back, panting. The sticky ooze coated her hair and smelled like piss. She was laying in piss. She gagged.

"You okay, sis?"

"Yeah," she coughed, "I hate it here."

Donovan snorted.

"We all do. Let's go."

The pair scrambled to their feet, trying to keep their footing on the slippery meat of the ground. Donovan got his first and started forward. Mayline shambled after him, trying to stay upright. She yelped as she went to the ground once more.

Donovan turned to help her up, and the air was rent with the sounds of baying wolves. Donovan cursed and grabbed Mayline, hauling his sister to her feet and dragging her behind him as he ran up the incline.

Mayline followed, looking over her shoulder as if she could see the hounds finding their trail.

Suddenly, they reached the top of the incline and in front of them was an obsidian gate. A Hell Gate. Donovan dragged Mayline towards the Gate as he started babbling.

"We need to open it. I don't know where in your world it'll lead, but it's a way out. It opens with blood. I'd do it, but I'm dead, and I don't have blood. It's gonna have to be you, but you'll be fine."

Mayline forced herself to nod. He pushed her gently toward the gate. She allowed a fang to protrude and she slid the shard tooth across the edge of her wrist. Mayline held her hand over the center of the gate, allowing the blood to drip from her skin onto the gate.

They waited a moment before looking at each other.

"It's not working."

"No, it's not."

"Why is it not working?"

"I don't know!"

Tears started falling from Mayline's face. She was panicking. She bit into her arm again, using her opposite hand to squeeze more blood onto the gate. The portal was closed. The only Hell Gate for miles would not open no matter how much blood she spilled on it. Mayline shrieked in frustration through her desperate tears. She was stuck in Hell. She was well and truly trapped. All hope of escape had vanished.

Her brother put a hand on her shoulder, his own lip trembling. He may not have been the most affectionate person while he was alive, but he would

not wish this eternity on his dear sister.

"It's gonna be okay," he lied. "We'll find a

different way out, okay?" Mayline shook her head,

hands covering her face as she let out a guttural sob.

Suddenly, a wind-whipped his body around

like a rag doll. He was flung to the side, away from

Mayline. Her hair swirled around her face as she

looked up, sticking to her cheeks where her tears had

tracked down from her eyes.

"Donny!"

"Mayline!"

He tried to reach her, but the fire erupted from her feet and burned up her body. She screamed as the flames licked her flesh clean of her bones. Donovan lurched toward her, but his hands closed around the fire and he yelped, pulling away in shock. He reached again, but it was too late.

With a final scream, the fire consumed the rest of Mayline's body. Donovan clutched the ashes of his sister, his eyes welling up.

He let out a wail and collapsed over the ashes, sobbing. Behind him, the hounds of Hell bayed as his crying was heard.

Rachelle whirled around from listening to her companions argue about what to do next at the sound of crackling fire.

Flames erupted from the summoning circle, and a female figure lay curled up in a ball on the ground. Rachelle rushed over and skidded on her knees to reach the figure. Rae let out a sob and sprinted to the body and flung herself over her friend.

Mayline's shoulders were shaking, she was covered in ashes, and her face was soaked with tears.

"Mayline!" Jennifer cried and ran to the girl. Mayline wrapped her arms around Rae's body and sobbed.

"You're safe now, sweetie, you're safe.

Breathe, relax…" Jennifer soothed, petting the

Vampire's hair.

"No! Donny's still there! He's gonna get

caught!"

"Mayline," Jennifer said, "Calm down. Who is

Donny?"

"My brother! He was there, he was helping

me, and now he's gonna get caught, and I can't help

him!" It was hard to understand her through the sobs,

but Jennifer got enough of it to pull Mayline into her

arms along with Rae who was trapped in Mayline's

embrace already. Jennifer waved Alex over who

willingly took Mayline into his arms and lifted her up.

"We can't help your brother, sweetie, but we

can take you home," Jennifer said. Alex started

carrying Mayline out of the clearing.

Rachelle stood up and brushed off her pants.

As the others followed Alex to the van they had

rented, Rachelle picked up a pale of water and poured

it over the summoning circle. She erased the

protective circles with the sole of her shoe. She

picked up the candles and the platter, dumping the

blood and the heart into the bushes at the edge of the clearing.

Once everything was cleaned and cleansed, Rachelle looked up at the sky. She was a Demon. She was not meant for Heaven. But surely…

"Hey, Creator. If her brother helped save her, surely that means he's a good person, right? Forgiveness is kind of Your thing, according to Mayline. You should… You should forgive him too. I guess." Rachelle felt stupid talking to the air, or even talking to the Being that Mayline worshipped so quietly but fervently. She scratched her head and shook herself.

"Whatever."

She turned away and went to join the others in the car.

Donovan closed his eyes, waiting for the hounds to get him. He had no reason to run. He was stuck there anyway. Suddenly, everything went quiet. He tensed, sure the hounds were about to attack.

Nothing happened.

He slowly opened his eyes. What greeted him

was gold. Bricks of gold under his feet. He reached

out and touched the cold metal and flinched. It was

warm. Beneath his hand, the bricks seemed to

breathe. He could feel a soft pulsing, like a heartbeat,

under his fingertips. He lowered his head, closing his

eyes. Wherever he was, it was better than the puss

and flesh of the last place.

Someone cleared their throat politely.

Donovan looked up and saw a man dressed in a white

robe standing in front of him.

Behind the man was a giant door made of gold

carved to look like wooden planks. The accents were

a shining opal that shifted colors and glimmered with

stardust. The golden bricks led up to the gate and

stopped just before reaching it. The man smiled, a

halo of light around his head as he looked down at

Donovan.

"Hello, my son. Congratulations."

"Where am I?"

"You have been Saved, my son. Your sister's

friend, a woman with Demon's power in her heart,

prayed for your forgiveness. I am so sorry you had to

suffer. Welcome to Heaven."

Donovan took the man's proffered hand, tears

of relief and joy spilling with every blink. The golden

gate behind the Saint opened.

Donovan stepped through, holding the hand

of the fatherly Saint, and the Heavenly Gate closed

behind his tired soul.

End of Book 1.

Heavenly Gate, illustrated by Devin Nelson

Sneak-peak of Book 2: Gates of Heaven

The heat of the Tuscan sun beat down on the group unforgivingly. The five people walked slowly, accommodating the injured in their party. Mayline looked up to the sky, squinting against the golden light, her forehead gleaming with perspiration. The dry heat of the Tuscan countryside was cooler than in the southern states of America, but the strain of walking so far while supporting the injured Macalah was draining the Raceling's strength. Mayline turned to their guide and tried to focus.

"Stephano! How much farther until we reach

the city?" she asked, raising her voice to be heard from the back of the group. The silver haired German looked back at her and smiled, although his sweaty face showed the strain of the journey.

"Not far now! Firenze lies just beyond this hill! We should be there within the hour." he said, his German accent diluted by and acquired Italian twinge.

Ahead of her, Mayline heard Rachelle and Rae sigh with relief. The hill in question wasn't too high or steep, though stones and trees jutted out from the ground at random intervals. Mayline glanced at the sky again. The sun was sinking beyond the horizon. She cursed as the edge of the moon made an appearance on the opposite side of the sky. If they were outside the city after nightfall, their pursuers would be able to follow them much faster, most likely catching them before the next dawn.

"Macalah," Mayline hissed, tightening her grip on her friend's arm, "I really hate to ask this of you, but can we go a bit faster? The moon is rising, and we need to get Rae into the city before she changes." The injured girl groaned in pain and tried to quicken her pace. The long gash down her right leg started to bleed again through the crude bandages. The group slowly made their way up the hill, dodging jagged stones and tightly packed trees along their way.

And then, suddenly, they came out of a grove

of trees to see themselves on the hilltop, looking

down on the city of Florence, Italy. Mayline sighed in

relief as the red-roofed buildings and towering

churches came into view. They were safe.

A howl broke through the twilight lit sky,

followed by several others.

Not so safe yet, it seemed.

Stephano flung Macalah over his shoulder and

the Racelings took off at a dead sprint, desperate to

reach the safety of the Raceling city of Florence.

About the Author

Sydnee Alyse Nelson was teethed and milked on the classical art of literature. Nelson's parents had her and her two brothers listening to audio recordings of books like *Redwall* (Brian Jacques), *Little Women* (Louisa May Alcott), and *Eragon* (Christopher Paolini). With appetite wetted, Nelson proceeded to devour young adult fiction like *Artemis Fowl* and *Half-moon Investigations* (Eoin Colfer), horror novels like *Salem's Lot* (Stephen King), and absolute classics in the fantasy genre from *Lord of the Rings* (J. R. R. Tolkien) and *The Chronicles of Narnia* (C. S. Lewis).

From an early age, Nelson was making up stories in the backyard of her parent's home alongside her older brothers and scribbling in tiny journals pretending to be an author signing the book for her fans. For as long as she can recall, she has dreamed of sharing her stories with the world.

About the Book

Blood of the Sire is Nelson's first long term project to come to fruition. It has undergone numerous re-writes, edits, adjustments, and breakdowns. Mayline and her friends have seen more tears from Nelson than any other story in her rather large archive. However, on the verge of giving up entirely, Nelson's best friend pushed for more.

"I want to know what happens next."

These words became a mantra of sorts for Nelson as she learned how to write like a professional. She knew the end of the story, but even she wanted to know what happened next. So she started writing without an outline, wanting to see where the characters took their own lives outside of her mind. It took years, nearly a decade of writing on and off, but Nelson was finally satisfied with the beginning of Mayline's story.

And she can't wait to see what happens next.

Look forward to other works by Sydnee A. Nelson, coming soon:

The Raceling Chronicles Book 2: Gates of Heaven

Evil Endeavors

Deals of Devils

CPSIA information can be obtained
at www.ICGtesting.com
Printed in the USA
FSHW011240020319
56038FS